THE ELECTRIC CUPID

THE ELECTRIC CUPID

•

Mary Fanjoy Reid

AVALON BOOKS
THOMAS BOUREGY AND COMPANY, INC.
401 LAFAYETTE STREET
NEW YORK, NEW YORK 10003

© Copyright 1998 by Mary Fanjoy Reid
Library of Congress Catalog Card Number: 98-96332
ISBN 0-8034-9312-6
All rights reserved.
All the characters in this book are fictitious,
and any resemblance to actual persons,
living or dead, is purely coincidental.

PRINTED IN THE UNITED STATES OF AMERICA
ON ACID-FREE PAPER
BY HADDON CRAFTSMEN, BLOOMSBURG, PENNSYLVANIA

To Bob, for sharing his electricity with me.

And thanks to Davina and Ron for their invaluable electrical and dental advice.

Chapter One

Lindsey polished off the last of her hot dog, and tore open the bag of caramel corn she'd won at the wire ring toss.

"Hoo boy! Why didn't I become an electrician? These guys you work with are something else," said Rhonda, gazing lazily over at the bare-chested men lining up for the caber toss. "Too bad I'm married." She sighed with a grin.

Lindsey grunted between chews, closed her eyes, and tilted her face up toward the sun. A rivulet of pain throbbed along the base of her jaw. She ran her tongue along her teeth, wincing. It had been like this for a week now, with the pain, unfortunately, steadily worsening.

"You know, that caramel corn isn't doing your teeth any good," said Rhonda. "You still got that toothache?"

"I'm okay." Lindsey grimaced, and set the caramel corn aside. She knew she was being silly, that she should go see the dentist, but she was still clinging to that desperate hope that this ache in her jaw would gradually lessen and disappear, and that whatever was causing her this distress would miraculously cure itself.

"You're just going to make matters worse for yourself." Rhonda shook her head. "Why don't you just make an appointment with the dentist?"

"I hate dentists."

"You're *afraid* of them, you mean," observed Rhonda wryly.

Lindsey squared her shoulders and set her lips into a thin,

rigid line. "I am not *afraid* of dentists. It's just..." She made a face. "... having some stranger poking his fingers in my mouth doesn't exactly appeal to me—"

"Here you are!" boomed a voice behind them. "McGinty, we don't have any Elektron representatives in the three-legged race."

Lindsey squinted up at the paunch-bellied man. "Well, don't look at me, Harry." Her gaze shifted to the figure standing next to her boss. But the high afternoon sun glinting off the wide, lacquered WELCOME SOUTHEAST BOSTON ELECTRICIANS sign obscured her vision.

"And besides, I thought you had a bad back," she added teasingly.

"Oh. I'm not talking about me," said Harry, turning to Rhonda.

"Hey, count me out," said Rhonda, rising from the picnic bench. "I can hardly make it on two legs as it is."

"I'll give it a try," said the man next to Harry.

"Wonderful," harrumphed Harry. "The race starts in five minutes. Do Elektron proud, McGinty. Wire Less has a twenty-point lead—" Enthusiastic cheering and raucous applause sounded from the caber toss arena. Harry let out a rumbling sigh and rubbed the bald spot on the top of his head. "Make that a fifty-point lead."

"I already competed in the wire ring toss—"

"And you won, yes." He rested his hand on her shoulder, nodding. "I'm proud of you, McGinty, but you see, there's no one left to enter the three-legged race. Tim had to leave early to take his kid to some baseball tournament, and the other guys—" He pointed in the direction of the caber toss and gazed at Lindsey imploringly. "I need you, McGinty. Elektron needs you. You're our last hope."

"Well..." Lindsey winced, groping in her brain for an excuse—any excuse.

"And then, there's the blind light bulb twist, and the potato sack race—"

The Electric Cupid

"Forget it. I'm not jumping around in a burlap bag in this heat," said Lindsey. "As for screwing in light bulbs with a blindfold—"

"I guess you were right, Harry." The man turned to Harry, shrugging. "Women just aren't competitive."

Lindsey frowned, shading her eyes as she turned to the speaker. "Now that's a load of hooey."

"Hooey?" The man smirked. "Even if I pretended to know what that means, I say the facts speak for themselves." He gazed out at the game field. "I mean, you don't see too many women competing out there, do you?"

"Only because we're outnumbered," said Lindsey tartly. "But that doesn't mean we're not competitive."

Out of the corner of her eye she glimpsed Sandra Goodman from Wire Less. The woman waved at her, fanning herself with a program schedule. She shifted her body awkwardly in a lawn chair, caressing her swollen, extended stomach. Sandra was an excellent electrician who'd been in the business a few years longer than Lindsey. The last two previous Electricians' Fairs, Sandra and Lindsey had gone head-to-head competing in the wire toss, and up until an hour ago, Sandra had twice been Wire Ring Toss Champion. But then last summer she'd suddenly gotten married, and now she was in no shape to compete, what with a child on the way....

Lindsey's attention was caught by Lisa Turnbull, another Wire Less employee—or rather, apprentice. The lithe woman was wearing a tiny bikini, lazily sunning herself on a towel on the grass. As far as Lindsey could tell, she hadn't moved from that spot since early this morning.

Flanking Lisa's left was a woman Lindsey didn't recognize. The woman wore dark sunglasses and a wide-brimmed hat, and she was busy lacing her long, slender arms with sunscreen. From where Lindsey sat, the woman appeared to have no color, her alabaster whiteness seeming to cleave through the hot early July heat like a graceful ice sculpture set amidst a crowd of sweating picnickers.

"Who is that—?" But Lindsey turned to see Rhonda already sneaking across the lawn to watch the caber toss. Her friend glanced back, gave her a smile, and waved.

"Okay, then." Harry consulted his watch. "You and Max had better hurry over there. The race starts in a couple of minutes."

Lindsey shook her head. "I'm not—"

"Afraid to compete?" Harry's companion flashed her a white-toothed smile. "Or are you afraid you can't keep up with me?"

Her retort was edged with sarcasm: "Hmmm... I'll try." She stood, and brushed hot-dog bun crumbs from her shorts. "After all, I'm just a woman; competing isn't something we women do well."

Before Harry's friend could reply, Lindsey was already making her way over to the three-legged race.

The announcer acknowledged Lindsey with a nod of his head. "O-okay!" he announced into his microphone. "Folks, it seems we have a last-minute team from Elekton joining us. Lindsey, the Wire Ring Toss Champion, and..." He gazed at her teammate.

Lindsey felt her face grow hot. "Er, this is—"

"Max," her teammate said, and he reached across Lindsey to shake the announcer's hand.

"Lindsey and Max!" the announcer finished with a smile. He reached behind him and handed them two pieces of rope.

"No electrician's tape this year?" Lindsey fingered the rope, untying some of the knots.

"Everyone complained about the tape stripping the hair off their legs." The announcer grinned.

"You wouldn't have to worry about that," Max observed, his eyes wandering appraisingly over her legs.

Lindsey bristled indignantly. "Listen, if you want—"

"... one leg each, tied together of course. If the rope comes untied, you are disqualified. No hopping, no spitting, no cursing. Keep it clean, folks," said the announcer, his voice raking loudly through the now-milling crowd. "And above all, let's have fun out there!"

Lindsey rolled her eyes and moved to the starting line. The other contestants were in the midst of securing their legs together.

"Right, or left?" asked her teammate.

"Right—er, left." She went to the other side of him.

She felt his thigh press against hers, and a sudden tingling sensation rippled up along her leg. She blinked, then recoiled, feeling suddenly as if she'd just received an electric shock.

"Well, we can't tie our legs together if you're over there," he said, raising his eyebrows.

Lindsey stared back at the hazel-brown eyes, taking in the high, smooth forehead, the strong aquiline nose. Her eyes were immediately drawn to the cleft in his chin, which deepened as he returned her stare with wry amusement, a taunting look in his expression.

"I'll do the tying," she said, snatching the other rope from his grasp.

She could feel him watching her as she looped the rope around their ankles. As she proceeded to bind their legs together, a sudden warmth flooded into her face. She fumbled with the knot, and even through the material of his jeans her fingers could not manage to avoid the hard muscles of his leg.

"Here, let me," and he ran his hands along the rope and around her leg, drawing it tight.

He grinned at her. "I don't make you nervous, do I?"

Lindsey straightened, compressing her lips. "No, not at all," she lied.

"Should we practice a little first?"

"Contestants get ready!" shouted the announcer.

"I guess we'll just go on instinct," he said, putting his arm around her waist.

"Do you mind?" She shrugged off his arm.

"This is going to be tough if you don't cooperate." He took her left arm and circled it about his waist. "Good thing we're the same height. I don't think I've ever run the three-legged race with a woman who's five-foot-eleven."

"I'm five-foot-nine and a half."

"Hmmm . . . or as long-legged as you," he observed, his eyes twinkling impishly at her.

Lindsey averted her gaze, furious at herself for flushing. She pursed her lips in concentration. "Left first, then right, right?"

"Right? You mean *my* right? *Or your* right?"

"On your mark, get set . . ."

"Your right, my left—" instructed Lindsey just as the pop of the gun echoed behind them.

Her teammate started forward on his free leg as Lindsey began with their bound legs. They teetered sideways, Lindsey's hand instinctively tightening around his waist.

"*Your* right," she growled under her breath, regaining her balance.

He gave a quick nod of understanding, and began to move with her: their tied-together legs, then the free leg, their tied legs, the free leg . . .

They picked up speed, striding almost effortlessly, seamlessly, as if they were one person. They passed a couple on their left who bumbled along, stumbled, and fell. Another pair petered out behind them, then another. Ahead of them loomed the leaders, and Lindsey ignored the hollering around them and instead concentrated on their pacing. She could hear her breath catching in her throat as their pace quickened into a swift loping gait. The fingers clasping her waist tightened and Lindsey felt her body pressing against the taut body of her teammate. They were in step with the leaders now.

When they crossed the finish line, Lindsey glanced quickly over her right shoulder to see the leaders less than half a stride behind them. But her teammate's abrupt halt jerked her backward, and Lindsey lost her balance, rebounding back into him like a rubber band.

She felt herself falling, and her hand flailed wildly, managing to clamp down on his bicep. But her teammate, taken by surprise by her sudden clumsiness, was unable to right himself in time, and she fell with a thud on top of him.

"And we have the winners of the three-legged race!" called the announcer. "Lindsey and Max... from Elektron!"

Max grinned at her, his face so close to hers Lindsey could feel his breath on her cheek. "I guess I should introduce myself: Hi, I'm Max Rupert." He extended his hand with a grunt.

Lindsey regarded his hand for a moment, then grudgingly accepted it. "Lindsey McGinty," she said, rolling off him. She sat up. Her heart was beating fast and hard in her chest—faster and harder than it should be.

Moving with some difficulty, he pulled himself up to a sitting position. "Gee, wanna do that again?"

"The race? Or the fall?"

"Hmm... that's a tough one." He stroked his chin, his hazel-brown eyes gazing at her with a mischievous glint.

Lindsey began untying the ropes. "Well, I think I proved my point."

"Oh? And exactly what point were you trying to prove?"

"That—" She broke off with a wince, hissing between her teeth as a wave of pain washed up the left side of her face. Her hand went to her cheek.

"Are you okay? I didn't hurt you, did?"

"No—"

"That was quite a race," said a female voice.

Lindsey glanced up at the woman, blinded for a moment

by the delicate pallor of her skin. Like a porcelain ballerina, she fluttered her long slender arm and took off her sunglasses and adjusted the wide brim of her hat. Long strawberry blond hair cascaded prettily across her shoulders, and Lindsey noticed the emerald shade of her dress matched her eyes, eyes that were staring intently down at her.

Lindsey passed a self-conscious hand over her short pixie-cut hair. "Hello."

"Hello," the woman answered tepidly.

Max greeted the woman with a casual smile. "Charlene Waters, this is McGinty, uh—"

"Lindsey. Lindsey McGinty." She started to rise, but suddenly realized her leg was still bound to Max's. Quickly, she reached over and began fumbling with the knot.

"Max, you ready to go?" said Charlene. "You promised to take me to the Museum of Fine Arts." Her voice carried in its cool, composed tone a twinge of querulousness.

The last knot finally sprung loose, and Max and Lindsey rose to their feet at the same time. They wiped the bits of grass from their clothes, Lindsey struggling to keep herself from glancing over at her teammate. But he took hold of her hand and gave it a quick squeeze.

"We make a pretty good team, Lindsey and I. Don't you think, Charlene?"

Charlene donned her sunglasses, smiling a bored, distant smile.

A carnivorous smile, thought Lindsey.

"We really should be going, Max," said Charlene, her lips drawing back slightly. "It was . . . nice to have met you, Lindsey."

Lindsey could feel the woman scrutinizing her, those emerald catlike eyes summing her up behind the dark glasses.

"McGinty! Max! Great race!" Harry slapped Lindsey on the back and shook Max's hand. "We're just ten points behind Wire Less. Mike and Sam just gained us some extra points in the archery contest. Now, if you can win the blind light bulb twist—"

"Harry, I'm done for the day," said Lindsey, stifling a groan as she felt another stab of pain shoot across the left side of her face.

"Well, it was fun racing with you," said Max. He paused suddenly, and frowned, gazing at Lindsey with concern. "Are you all right?"

Lindsey forced a cheerful expression into her face. "Me? I'm fine."

"Tough as nails, my McGinty is," said Harry, leading her through the dispersing crowd. "She's going to help me win the trophy this year."

"Harry—"

"See ya later, Max, Charlene!" He waved at them. "Hey, and thanks!" He guided Lindsey toward a man with a clipboard. "Another entry for the blind light bulb twist," he told the man. "McGinty, Lindsey—for Elektron."

"Starts in three minutes." The man scribbled her name onto the list.

Harry rubbed her shoulders, making Lindsey feel like a horse about to begin a race. "You're not too tired, are you? Ah, what's thirty light bulbs? You're one of my best electricians; you can do it in your sleep, even blindfolded. Speaking of which—" He held up the black cloth. His forehead creased as he gazed at her. "Hey, you look a little out of it." Harry eyed her worriedly. "You feeling okay?"

Lindsey snatched the blindfold from his hand and glowered at him. "I'm fine." She pursed her lips. "Just too much sun, I guess."

"Well, win this, McGinty, and I'll buy you one of those huge caramel apples."

Lindsey grinned despite the ache in her jaw. "I'd settle for a raise."

"I'm already going broke as it is. How about a vacation instead?"

The man with the clipboard cleared his throat over the microphone. A murmuring started through the crowd.

"Go on now. Do me proud." He glanced at his watch. "And hurry up, will ya? The potato sack race starts in fifteen minutes."

"Who was that incredibly handsome hunk you were falling all over?" asked Rhonda, climbing into the passenger seat of the truck.

Lindsey shrugged. "Some friend of Harry's. And I wasn't 'falling all over him.' "

"Hmmm... could've fooled me." Rhonda clicked in her seat belt, and reached up to check her earrings. "Oh, no! I lost another one." She groaned in frustration, feeling around the seat. "Whew! Here it is!" She held up the long dangling earring.

"I don't know how you can wear those things." Lindsey shook her head and started the truck. "I'm surprised your earlobes haven't fallen off yet."

"It's my fashion statement." She hooked the earring into her lobe. "You know, like Jackie Kennedy and her pillbox hat—speaking of which, who was that woman you were talking to? The one with the designer hat. Not the guy's wife, I hope."

Charlene Waters. "I don't know. Maybe." Lindsey shrugged. But she hadn't spied a wedding band on Max's finger.

"So what does this guy do? Is he an electrician, too?"

"I don't know." But Lindsey doubted this man worked in the electricial trade. For one, his fingernails were too clean. And there was a scent about him—a different smell, the smell of management, maybe.

"You don't even know what he does for a living?" Rhonda sighed. "Lin, I've got to teach you the art of conversation. How're you going to meet anyone if you don't put yourself out? I think I know more about your coworkers than you do." She gave her friend a sly look. "Did you know Mike Renowski is single? He's kind of handsome, too—"

"Rhonda, he's a coworker. I don't date people I work with." Lindsey honked at a black van that cut her off. She cursed under her breath, and let out a loud "Aaghhh!" as a ribbon of pain seared across her left cheek. She grimaced, waiting for the pain to subside.

"So, he's asked you out?"

"Who?"

"Mike Renowski! Are you listening to me?" Rhonda cocked a frustrated eyebrow at her friend. But her expression immediately softened when she glimpsed Lindsey's pained grimace. "Hey, your tooth still bothering you?"

"It'll go away." Lindsey grunted. She turned off the highway and eased onto Commonwealth Street, shaking her head at the congested traffic.

"You should've seen Mike's face when you and that guy fell on top of each other. I'm telling you, that guy likes you, Lindsey."

"What guy?"

Rhonda exhaled loudly, shaking her head. "Am I having a one-way conversation here? Mike! I'm talking about Mike!"

"Oh," said Lindsey.

"Who'd you think I was talking about? Wait a minute— you didn't think I was referring to Harry's friend there, uh—what was his name?"

"Max. Max Rupert," said Lindsey, without thinking. She could feel Rhonda's inquisitive eyes boring holes into the side of her head.

"Well," Rhonda spoke up after a moment, "he was quite attractive—and if you say 'who?' again, I'll throttle you."

Lindsey chewed on her lip. "His girlfriend was quite attractive, as well."

"You don't know if that was his girlfriend. For all you know she could be his sister, a cousin, or something."

"Rhonda, can you stop trying to make something out of nothing? I-I don't even know the guy." She veered down Fuller Street and nosed in behind the white Camry parked in the driveway.

"You know, you're still welcome to come to Hawaii with Rick and me. I hear the beach is crawling with handsome Antonio Banderas look-alikes just waiting for a single, attractive woman like you to come along—"

"Didn't you tell me this trip was kind of like a belated honeymoon for you two? I'd only be in the way," said Lindsey. "Besides, I have to work."

"Harry told me you didn't put in for vacation time again this year." Rhonda hopped out of the truck. "What are you trying to do? Work yourself to death? You're thirty-two years old, Lindsey. This is a time when you should be out there enjoying yourself—have fun for a change! I mean, how long has it been since you went out on a date?"

Lindsey chewed on her lip. *Too long*, she thought.

"And it's not as if there aren't any contenders." Rhonda shot her a coy look. "Take Mike, for example."

"You know my rule about not dating coworkers," reminded Lindsey. Just last month she'd turned down Mike, using this explanation (or was it an excuse?) when he'd asked her to the Annual Electricians' Ball.

Rhonda sighed, shaking her head in defeat. "Well, there's always what's his name who lives below you."

"Lenny?" Lindsey snorted, not even dignifying this suggestion with a reply.

"Anyway, we still on for Saturday?"

Lindsey nodded. "Sure." She waved as Rhonda shut the truck door.

On her way home, Lindsey found her mind beginning to drift, alternating between the throbbing ache in her jaw and the events of the day.

Like last year, they'd lost the trophy to Wire Less, despite Lindsey winning both the blind light bulb twist and the potato sack race. During the trophy ceremony she'd been unusually distracted, her gaze wandering restlessly over the crowd. She realized only in hindsight what she was doing—she was searching for *him*, her mysterious three-legged race teammate: Max Rupert.

And it had taken everything in her to restrain herself from asking Harry about this man. Who was Max Rupert? She was curious to know. Already she'd deduced he wasn't an electrician. Perhaps an administrator? An accountant? Harry's new business manager?

And yet, somehow, from Lindsey's first impression of Max Rupert, none of these job descriptions seemed to fit him. And she'd noticed he didn't speak with that clipped Bostonian accent, either. Where was he from then? And who was that woman with him? What was her name? Charlene?

Immediately upon being introduced to the woman, Lindsey'd sensed the signals: a kind of territoriality, a possessiveness that clearly warned: "Hands off; he's mine."

Were Max Rupert and this woman romantically involved? she wondered as she parked her Toyota behind the shark-gray Camaro in the driveway. Oh, but what did it matter, anyway; it wasn't likely she'd be running into Max Rupert again.

Her hand went to her left thigh, feeling the phantom warmth of his leg against hers. Something about that man . . .

She immediately scoffed at herself and slid out of the truck. Rhonda was right; she really should get out and meet more people. And it wasn't as if no one was asking her out—

"Hey-ho! Lindsey girl!" Lenny Bryce strode out from the back door, hitching up his jeans.

"Hi, Lenny. How's tricks?"

"Tricks are fine. That is, they would be if you'd just go out with me." He crossed the lawn and fell into step with her up the front walkway. "Hey, I've got two pork chops defrosting right now on my kitchen counter—and a nice bottle of Mexican Chianti just waiting to be opened. So how about it?" He leered a smile at her.

"Thanks, Lenny. But tonight I think I'll just stay home and watch the tube."

"Want some company? I hear the Undertaker's battling Brett 'the Hit Man' Heart tonight."

Lindsey sighed. "As exciting as that sounds, I think I'm going to have to pass," she said, fitting her key into the front door.

"Or we can watch the ball game. No? How about a movie, then? There's this Chuck Norris flick on at eight...."

Lindsey finally managed to open the door and she waved at him without turning, closing the door behind her.

No, it wasn't as if no one was asking her out—just the *wrong* people, she thought with a sigh as she hung her purse on the hat rack and slumped down on her couch.

Chapter Two

Lindsey stared at her reflection, and gingerly prodded the left side of her face. She winced as this action produced another wave of pain. *Oh, great!* she thought miserably. *I look like a chipmunk storing nuts—in one cheek.*

She glanced back down at the open phone book, and with a surrendering sigh, she dialed the number she'd circled.

"Good morning. Dr. Grable's office," a woman answered cheerfully.

"Hello. This is, er, Lindsey..." She flexed her lips, trying to enunciate her words over the swelling. "This is Lindsey McGinty. I seem to be, er, having a slight problem with my tooth." *Or teeth*, she added with a silent grimace. "I don't have an appointment—"

"I'm afraid Dr. Grable is on vacation, Ms. McGinty. But if it's an emergency I can refer you to another dentist."

An emergency? Lindsey squinted at the woman in the mirror. The pain was more than a week old, but the dull ache had in the past couple of days grown increasingly persistent, now localizing with searing accuracy in the lower left side of her jaw. Why hadn't she taken Rhonda's advice and gone to see the dentist sooner? she chastised herself.

"Emergency? Er, yes, I guess you could call it that. My cheek is pretty swollen," she told the receptionist.

Lindsey could hear the light tapping of a keyboard in the background. "I'm sorry. You said, Lindsey McGinty?"

"Yes."

"I can't seem to locate your file."

"It's, er, been a while since I've been in," Lindsey confessed sheepishly. *About sixteen years to be exact*, she added silently.

"I'll let them know you're coming in this morning, Ms. McGinty," assured the receptionist, after reciting the dentist's address over the phone.

Lindsey nodded into the receiver. "Thank you. Oh! You, er, didn't give me—" She heard the click in her ear, and then the dial tone. "—the dentist's name." Lindsey sighed and rang off.

She phoned Harry at work and told him she wouldn't be in until later.

"Bad tooth, huh? Tell him to just yank it out. Had a couple of teeth just filled last month. Hurt like crazy," he growled.

"Thanks, Harry. I really needed to hear that."

"Huh. Some coincidence—I mean, you meeting Max Rupert yesterday."

"Coincidence?" Lindsey frowned, cradling the phone receiver between her cheek and shoulder blade as she slipped her feet into her work boots. She waited for her boss to elaborate. What about this man, Max Rupert?

But Harry only cleared his throat and told her he'd send Mike to do the job in Dorchester. "You take it easy. That anesthetic stuff'll probably knock you for a loop for most of the day, anyway."

Anesthetic? She compressed her lips together firmly, which emerged as a pouty, lopsided half-grin. "Harry, I'm not going in for surgery. I'll be in this afternoon—if not earlier."

"Tough girl, huh? Okay, McGinty, but I don't want to end up playing nursemaid—"

"I'll be in," Lindsey repeated gruffly. "Just because I'm a woman—"

"Oh-ho! McGinty, I don't think of you as a woman. To me, you're just one of the guys."

"Thanks." Lindsey poked her cheek, and was instantly rewarded with a fireball of pain that lashed up the side of her face. "I think," she added with a muffled groan, and hung up.

She combed her fingers through her pixie-cut hair, and rolled her coveralls into her knapsack. She glanced at the address she'd written down. The dental office was in the South End of Boston, not too far from Elektron Hardware & Contracting Services.

No problem, she thought; once the dentist managed to get rid of this swelling—and determine the cause of it—she'd swing back to work.

Lindsey drew in a deep breath, pushing her hands against her stomach, trying to calm the queasy knots beginning to twist inside. What was it about dentists that frightened her so?

She retreated into the bathroom and splashed cold water on her face, catching a glimpse of her chipmunk cheek. Maybe if she left it alone it'd go away, she rationalized hopefully as she scrutinized her reflection. She pressed the heel of her hand to her cheek, as if attempting to flatten the swelling.

"Aaah!" She gasped, sucking in air between her teeth as this action sent another jolt of pain.

She straightened, blinking back the sharp ache in her jaw, and gazed at her reflection square in the eye. "Okay, Lindsey McGinty. You've got a problem. Deal with it. You are a strong, mature woman. You are not afraid of the dentist."

However, as she veered her Toyota onto Highway 90 and made her way toward Boston's South End, the quivery sensation in her belly only grew stronger.

She gripped the wheel tightly, struggling in vain to shrug off her apprehension. And for a moment, the fearful cramping in her stomach took her mind away from the throbbing ache in her jaw. Once again, that clinging hope behind her rational brain leaped to the forefront of her thoughts, deluding her into believing that by the time she reached the dental office, the pain and swelling would have subsided, and that whatever was causing it would have miraculously cured itself.

As Lindsey pushed through the glass doors of the dental office, however, she knew she was in trouble. Her head lolled like a pumpkin, the pain now tearing up above her eyes, leaving the base of her left ear to pulse with a burning ache.

She approached the front desk. "Hello, I'm Lindsey McGinty—" She suddenly stopped short as the woman sitting behind the computer turned to look at her.

Even without the hat and sunglasses, Lindsey instantly recognized that porcelain beauty. "Oh. Hello. Er . . . Charlene, isn't it?"

The receptionist's smile faded slightly as her green, catlike eyes flickered in momentary acknowledgment. "The woman from the Electricians' Fair." The dismissiveness in her tone immediately brought back that same self-consciousness Lindsey'd felt yesterday when she'd been introduced to this woman.

"Dr. Grable's office told us a patient of theirs was coming in," said Charlene. "I see you've got . . ." The corners of her lips bunched together. ". . . some swelling."

"Yes, I—"

"The dentist is with a patient at the moment, Mrs. McGinty. If you can't wait—"

"It's all right. I-I can wait." She grimaced; surely the pain couldn't get any worse.

"Well." Charlene gazed at her uncertainly. "He'll be out shortly." She turned her back on Lindsey, and reached into the filing cabinet, extracting some forms.

"I'll need you to fill these out, Mrs. McGinty."

"Er, actually it's *Miss* McGinty," Lindsey corrected.

The receptionist hesitated, glancing down at the forms in her hands. Her manicured nails tapped the forms, pink-polished talons clicking against the paper. "Dr. Grable's office didn't seem to have a file on you. But you are a patient of Dr. Grable's?" To Lindsey, her words formed more a statement than a question.

"Er, well, I'm not actually a regular patient, if that's what you mean. It's been . . . a while since I've visited the dentist." Lindsey flushed as she proceeded to fill out the forms.

"Shall I transfer the information, then, back to Dr. Grable?" Charlene smiled. But there was wariness in the receptionist's expression.

Lindsey gazed at the woman, taking in the pristine, almost breakable beauty. Her strawberry blond hair was gathered into a neat chignon at the back of her long swanlike neck, the peppermint pink of her crisp, clean blouse offsetting the milky whiteness of her flawless skin.

"Well, it-it doesn't matter to me. I'm not really a patient of Dr. Grable's, but if that's what—"

She was interrupted by a loud guffaw. Lindsey turned to see a tall man in a white coat steering a burly patient out through the door next to the receptionist's desk.

"Now, I want you to try to stay away from those sweets, Earl. And remember to floss," said the tall man in the white coat.

Lindsey's heart skipped a beat as she recognized that voice—and now, as she stared at him, recognized the owner of that voice.

"How can I forget?" The burly patient rubbed his bearded face. "That assistant of yours really worked me over. Reminds me of my mother-in-law," he grumbled.

"In another life, our Mrs. Honeysuckle worked as a dental assistant for the U.S. Army." The tall man laughed.

"I was thinking more along the lines of drill sergeant," mumbled Earl, clasping the dentist's hand. "Thanks, Max. Don't take this the wrong way, but I hope I won't be seeing you anytime soon."

The dentist grinned. "Take care of those teeth is all I ask."

Earl glanced over at the receptionist. "Have a good day, Miss Waters." He nodded to Lindsey and winked. "Don't worry, dear. You're in safe hands with Dr. Rupert." He grinned. "It's that Sergeant Honeysuckle you have to watch out for." He rubbed his jaw and tromped out of the office.

Max Rupert turned to Lindsey, his expression suddenly contorting into a look of surprise. He blinked. "Hello." His eyebrows shot up and a wide smile broke out across his face. "Or, hello *again,* maybe I should say."

Lindsey stared, as if mesmerized, into the bright hazel-brown eyes. She felt him clasp her hand, and warmth flooded her swollen face. "Hi," she stammered. "I-I didn't know you were a—"

"Mrs. McGinty is a patient of Doctor Grable's," said Charlene.

"It's, er, *Miss* McGinty," said Lindsey. And she flushed at the quick rush of her correction, suddenly aware, also, of the way Max Rupert was gazing at her.

"Hmmm . . . I'd better take a look at that swelling," he said, frowning. He gently cupped her elbow and led her past the desk and through the door.

Lindsey gave the receptionist a sideways glance, and she couldn't be certain, but she thought she detected in the woman's pretty porcelain face a pinch of sudden disapproval.

As Lindsey stepped into the room, her stomach fluttered nervously. Max gestured to the chair and she obediently sat down. Her underarms were sticky with perspiration, and the muscles in her back pulled taut.

Lindsey swept a cursory glance about the clean white walls, her nostrils flaring at the disinfectant smells. Striving to compose herself, she let her gaze wander over the array of photographs displayed sporadically about the room. A few depicted forests and treelines, another showed off green misted hills with a shoddy looking cabin looming in the foreground. However, mostly the photographs were of water: clear, silver-blue ribbons, backed by forested and hilly horizons. In some, the stretch of water sparkled with sunlight; in others, moonbeams gleamed like tiny electric sequins. Lindsey found herself instantly drawn to them.

And then Lindsey's eyes came to rest on the last photograph behind her.

The man in the photograph was wearing a silly-looking hat, the ornamented brim flipped up to reveal a good-humored face with a high, broad forehead. The grin on the man's face was proud but modest as he posed for the person behind the camera. The fish he held up was enormous.

"Charlene's idea," said Max, following her gaze. "I think she feels I won't get homesick if I surround myself with all this memorabilia."

Lindsey nodded. It had taken her only a second to recognize the young woman in the photograph next to him; Charlene's hat and sunglasses could not conceal that porcelain pristineness.

"Oh, so you're not from Boston?" she said, although she'd already gathered this from their first meeting.

"I'm from New Brunswick, actually," he said, snapping on his latex gloves.

"New Brunswick, Canada?"

Max nodded. "But I was born right here in Boston. My folks moved to Saint Andrews when I was three." He sighed, gazing wistfully at the photographs. "I guess it's probably the fishing I miss the most. But Boston—Boston is where my roots are. And I'm really getting to like this city...." A twinkle appeared in his hazel-brown eyes as they fell back to her, observing her for a prolonged moment. "And the people," he added with a smile.

"We Bostonians are a crazy bunch," murmured Lindsey, smiling uneasily, "but you'll get used to us."

Her gaze flickered to the framed inscription above the doorway: *Healthy teeth are all alike; every unhealthy tooth is unhealthy in its own way.* Lindsey found herself chuckling quietly at this.

"I stole that from Tolstoy," said Max, staring at the inscription.

"*Anna Karenina*," Lindsey acknowledged with a nod. "I bet ol' Tolstoy is rolling over in his grave about now."

"Yes, well, I suppose he never suspected he'd be an inspiration to a dentist." Max grinned.

Lindsey laughed, and immediately grimaced as a stab of pain reeled across her jaw.

"How's the pain? Not too bad, I hope," he said with a sympathetic wince.

"I think my fear has lessened it for now," she mumbled, kneading her hands together. "Uh, I should tell you, I'm-I'm not that keen on dentists."

"Aw, but we've just met. You can't judge a man by his profession," he said with a teasing smile. "Wait until you get to know me, I'm not such a bad guy." He inclined his head, a mixture of amusement and curiosity crossing his handsome face. "I bet you get a lot of jokes about *your* profession."

Lindsey bristled. "About my being a *woman* electrician, you mean."

Before Max could respond, a stout woman appeared in the doorway. Her white uniform swished coarsely as she strode in, her brightly polished nurse's shoes squeaking against the linoleum. Everything about her, from the cropped gray hair to the deliberate set of her shoulders, said: *"I'm in charge, so don't give me any nonsense."*

She regarded Max over her horn-rimmed glasses, her lips

pursed, not disapprovingly, but with a look a mother might give a rambunctious child.

"Lindsey McGinty, this is my beautiful, most esteemed dental assistant, Mrs. Honeysuckle."

Mrs. Honeysuckle harrumphed and cocked an eyebrow at him, indicating that his flattery tactics weren't going to succeed in mellowing her one bit. And yet, Lindsey caught, too, the faint hint of a smile in her expression, a muffled spark of humor in the small blue eyes, and Lindsey felt herself taking an instant liking to this older woman.

"How long have you had that swelling, my dear?" she demanded, the small eyes behind the horn-rimmed spectacles peering at her, taking mental notes.

"I, er, woke up with it," replied Lindsey, feeling slightly ashamed now by her childish reluctance to have seen to her problem sooner.

As if reading her thoughts, Mrs. Honeysuckle gazed at her, tsk-tsking under her breath. "You young people. So busy working, you don't take the time to look after yourselves. Neglect your teeth and you'll be sorry. You think those teeth will last forever?"

Lindsey squeezed her hands into fists as sharp pain shot across the left side of her face. *You can take them all out, for all I care right now*, she groaned inwardly.

Max motioned for Lindsey to lie back in the chair. "Okay, let's see what's causing the problem here."

His fingers were gentle as they probed inside her mouth. Lindsey's gaze meandered over the straight, attractive brow, noting how the dark lashes curled up at the ends like a child's. Laugh lines parenthesized a wry mouth, and again she found herself drawn to the cleft in his chin which trembled slightly as his brow furrowed in concentration. As a tantalizing, spicy scent of musk wafted over her, Lindsey could feel her muscles untense a little, her fingers uncurling from her fists.

"Aha. There's the culprit," he said, nodding his head

slowly. In that instant his gaze moved to meet her own, and Lindsey flushed. Max smiled, and straightened.

He snapped off his gloves and sat down. "How attached are you to your wisdom tooth?"

"I don't know," said Lindsey, sitting up. "Having four of them hasn't made me any wiser. I suppose letting one of them go won't . . . hurt." Her smile was apprehensive.

Max chuckled softly. "Unfortunately, there's no such thing as painless dentistry. But I'm afraid your lower left molar has abscessed, which means it has to come out."

He looked at her seriously. "The good news is I don't see any visible nerve damage, but I'd have to take some X rays to be certain." His smile was grim. "But first, we have to get that swelling down."

"You should have been in to see Dr. Rupert earlier, young lady," said Mrs. Honeysuckle sternly. She pursed her lips and consulted her watch. "I'll go prepare a tray for the next patient, Dr. Rupert." She shook her head at Lindsey. "Such a pretty girl. It would be a shame to let those teeth go. Remember now to floss. Flossing is important." And she swooshed out of the room, her departure punctuated by a haze of motherly discipline that lingered long enough to make Lindsey feel half her age and properly chastised.

"Her bark's worse than her bite." Max grinned. He swiveled his chair over to his desk and opened a folder. He searched among the cubbyholes, moving about his papers until he found a pen.

"You don't have any allergies you're aware of?" he asked, glancing through the forms in the folder.

Lindsey shook her head. "Oh, well, I am allergic to mustard." She clasped her fingers together nervously. "But that's about it."

"You're not allergic to any mediations? Penicillin?"

"No."

"Good. I'm going to prescribe some amoxicillin to clear

up that infection." He reached for a pink pad and scribbled some words. "It'll help with the pain and the swelling. But you'll have to take the amoxicillin for at least seven days."

"So, this means . . . I have to come back?"

Max noted her stricken look, and gave her a half sympathetic, half teasing smile. "You don't want to see me again?"

Lindsey could feel her face growing hot, and she was furious at herself for reacting to his obvious playful teasing. If only he weren't so good-looking. . . .

"Now, with this medication I must inform you of a few precautions." He launched into a list of information, and Lindsey found herself hypnotized by the soothing sound of his voice.

"Lindsey? Did you hear me?"

Lindsey struggled to keep herself from blushing. "Sorry," she murmured, swinging her legs over the side of the dentist chair. "I, er, really have to get back to work," she said.

Max looked up, watching her for a brief moment. A glint appeared in his hazel-brown eyes and his lips curved into an amused, curious smile. "Maybe you'd better take the day off. Wait until that swelling and pain subside a little."

"It's-it's not that bad, really." But even as she said this a needle of pain ricocheted up from where his fingers had probed her mouth.

He regarded her, frowning. "The pain should subside in a couple of days. But if it gets too much for you to handle, you can try some regular Tylenol. Or, if you'd like, I could prescribe some Tylenol 3—"

"Thank you," said Lindsey, throwing back her shoulders rigidly, "but I think I can handle it."

Max's eyebrows lifted. "Oh, I forgot. You're a tough electrician—a *competitive* woman," he added with a ghost of a smirk.

What's wrong with my being competitive? "For your information, there are other women who are just as competitive as me." Her words edged on curtness, a defensive note climbing into her tone. "I'm really not all that... unique."

"Well, I wouldn't say that." His eyes swept over her rumpled T-shirt and jeans, pausing to rest on her work boots.

Lindsey took the pink slip from his hand. "Thanks." She half-sighed, ignoring his grin.

"We'll make an appointment for next Monday, then? If that's convenient?" He rose from his chair.

Lindsey gazed into his handsome face, suddenly unnerved by the way his hazel-brown eyes held her own dark brown ones. An odd tingling sensation was rippling up her left leg, and her chest suddenly constricted. She quickly averted her eyes, slipping off the chair. Max didn't move away.

"Monday. Sure," she mumbled, self-consciously tucking her T-shirt into the waistband of her shorts. "The sooner I get rid of this tooth, the better."

Max nodded. "Sometimes it's best to deal with a situation before it becomes an even bigger problem."

"Yes," Lindsey confessed sheepishly, "I—I thought maybe if I just ignored it, the tooth would just..." She grimaced, touching her cheek.

"Dentists aren't the bad guys, you know," said Max. "We're supposed to make your life easier."

Easier? Lindsey's pulse quickened, but not with fear, she realized. For some reason, this man's close proximity was doing something to her nervous system. It was as though she were fighting some irresistible force, a magnetic pull that was drawing her toward him. She took a step back, trying to suppress this sudden excitement stirring inside her. But her face glowed warmly and the palms of her hands, she noted with dismay, were sweating.

"I'll tell Charlene to set up the appointment, then—"

The Electric Cupid 27

"Everything all right in here?" The receptionist stood in the doorway. Her green, catlike eyes shifted from Max to Lindsey.

"Ah, perfect timing." Max grinned. "Charlene, you already know Lindsey. I was just going to ask you to set up an extraction for next Monday."

Charlene's delicate brows drew together. "Mrs. McGinty is Dr. Grable's patient—"

"It's *Miss* McGinty, isn't it?" Max turned to Lindsey.

Lindsey nodded. "Actually, I'm not really a regular patient of Dr. Grable's—" she began, embarassed. *Not since I was sixteen, in fact.*

"Well, then, they won't mind if we steal you away from them," said Max. "And it's not as if we have a patient overload." This last comment was directed to Charlene.

"But—" The receptionist cut herself off and compressed her lips, staring at Max.

Mrs. Honeysuckle arrived carrying a tray of dangerous-looking instruments. She swished past Charlene, shooting Lindsey a matronly, no-nonsense look above her horn-rimmed spectacles.

"Now, Miss McGinty. You be sure and get that prescription filled." She gestured to the pink slip in Lindsey's hand. "And follow Dr. Rupert's instructions."

"Which includes giving me a call if any other problems should arise in the meantime." Max grinned. He extracted a business card from his coat pocket, taking a moment to scribble something on the bottom. He handed the card to her. "That's my home phone number."

Lindsey caught the swift look of the receptionist, the harshness of her frown marring for an instant the delicate porcelain features. A new tension suddenly seeped into the room as Charlene narrowed her eyes at Lindsey, then relayed a not-so-subtle message of displeasure to Max. Lindsey glanced down at the card in her hands, feeling as though she'd stumbled, uninvited, into some kind of private conversation.

However, neither Max nor Mrs. Honeysuckle seemed to have picked up on this sudden burgeoning tension—or its source: this pretty receptionist whose eyes were now regarding Lindsey with open dislike.

"I'll, er, see you in a week, then," Lindsey muttered, striding past the receptionist. She shivered a little beneath Charlene's chilly smile.

And yet, as she climbed into her Toyota truck, she could feel a strange warmth uncoiling inside her. And after a moment, she realized she was smiling.

You've just been to the dentist, and you're smiling? She shook her head in wonderment. *And don't forget you have to come back in a week.*

But much to her surprise, this thought filled her with none of the expectant anxiety or apprehension. Instead, she found that a tiny part of her was actually looking forward to her next appointment with Dr. Max Rupert.

Lindsey paused to stare at her reflection in the rearview mirror and was astonished by what she saw. Despite her chipmunk cheek, her dark brown eyes were shining, and her face was flushed a warm pink. Her full lips curved into a lopsided smile, a smile of excitement and anticipation—a *flirtatious* smile, she noticed in bewilderment.

And then, another painful wave crashed up into the left side of her face, and the reality of her situation pierced through her thoughts. She glanced down at the pink slip crumpled in her hand. Max's business card fluttered between the gearshift. After a moment, she retrieved it and with a deliberate motion, Lindsey tossed it up on the dashboard.

So he gave you his home phone number. It didn't mean anything; he's new in town, and you're his new patient with a bad tooth.

She pulled out of the parking lot with a moan, and cursed

her abscessed wisdom tooth for getting her into this situation—

What situation? she retorted to herself. If she'd dealt with this problem sooner—

Well, no sense dwelling on it, she told herself firmly. She reversed out of the driveway and made her way toward the pharmacy, absently rubbing her left leg, as if this action might force out the lingering presence of Max Rupert. But his spicy, musky aftershave still filled her nostrils, and those penetrating hazel-brown eyes and teasing grin of his had annoyingly emblazoned themselves in her mind.

Despite Lindsey's protests, Harry had sent her home early.

"I've booked you for a lone job on Wednesday. Just a panel upgrade for a home up in Cambridge. Tomorrow, I'm sending you to help with the fluorescent lighting job at the Children's Museum."

"I could go to Dorchester and help Mike—"

"He can handle it, McGinty." Harry smiled, frustrated. "You're not the only competent electrician here." The phone buzzed, and he picked it up, massaging his temples.

Lindsey rose from the chair as Christine swept in with a stack of files. She dumped them on Harry's desk, ignoring the burly man's sour look.

"Hey, Lindsey," she greeted tiredly, then winced as she noted Lindsy's swollen cheek. "Oooh. What happened to you?"

"Bad tooth," said Lindsey, gingerly touching the left side of her face.

Christine gazed at her sympathetically. "Hmmm . . . I have a good dentist for you. I just took my kids in the other day. His name is Rupert—Max Rupert. The kids just loved him. He's new to the area—from somewhere up in Canada—"

"New Brunswick." Lindsey nodded. "Yes, he's my—"

She hesitated, feeling her cheeks growing warm all of a sudden. "I went to see him this morning," she said quickly.

Christine's smile broadened. "Quite a hunk, isn't he? And he's not married."

"Christine, can you get me the Beckham Automotive file?" Harry interrupted gruffly, his big red hand covering the other end of the receiver. "McGinty, you still here? Go home! Relax for once in your life! That cheek of yours is starting to give me an even bigger headache." He rubbed the the bald spot on his head with a grimace.

"He's such a sweet boss, isn't he?" Christine rolled her eyes.

Lindsey laughed and glanced at her watch: 2:30. She waved at Harry, who acknowledged it with a dismissive nod of his head.

As she strode toward her truck, Lindsey felt oddly restless. Thoughts bombarded her head, distracting her, causing tiny jolts of excitement to flutter about in the pit of her stomach. So now she knew for a fact that Dr. Max Rupert wasn't married. And this new information made her heart beat all the more faster.

So what if he wasn't married? He was just her dentist, after all. But as she climbed into her truck, her eyes were inevitably drawn to the business card on the dashboard. Did he give out his personal phone number to all his clients? Lindsey wondered.

She clicked on the radio and veered her truck toward home. From the speakers Etta James crooned about love that finally appears after a long wait. . . .

Lindsey snapped off the radio, and at the last minute swerved down Lincoln Street, heading toward the downtown area. She might as well take advantage of her spare time and visit that antique bookstore she'd long been meaning to check out.

Some weeks ago she'd spied a book about Thales of

Miletus displayed in the front window. Rhonda had been with her and wanted to stop and look at an old seventies edition of *How to Meet the Man of Your Dreams*.

"Come on, Lin. I'll buy it for you," her friend had urged.

"Forget it, Rhonda. I don't need a book to tell me how to meet a man."

Lindsey's hands tightened on the steering wheel, and she sighed aloud. No, she already knew how to meet the "man of her dreams": first, allow yourself to be coerced into running the three-legged race with a complete stranger, let your wisdom tooth abscess, then let this same stranger become your dentist.

But he's just your dentist, Lindsey, she reminded herself. *Regardless of whether he's a "dish" or not.*

And with a determined grimace, she shrugged away these thoughts of Max Rupert, and focused on Thales of Miletus, a mathematician and experimenter with electricity who couldn't possibly rise from the dead to distract her—or complicate her life any further.

Chapter Three

Lindsey spent the morning flipping through the thick tome she'd found at the antique bookstore. Much to her disappointment, the biography of Thales of Miletus had already been sold—

"Funny thing, miss. You're the second person to ask after that book today. And it's been sitting in that window for months," the clerk told her. "A gentleman came in and just bought it less than an hour ago."

But the book she'd ended up buying, *Echoes of Magnetism and Electricity*, was equally as fascinating, and as expensive—though it was worth it, if not merely for the photographs depicting prototypical lightning rods and capacitors. The editors had also included a fully detailed plan of the Leyden jar, and a lengthy section devoted to William Gilbert, who was hired on as personal physician to Queen Elizabeth I, and who was the first person to use the word *electric*.

Lindsey paused to gaze at the drawing of Gilbert's sixteenth-century "vesorium," a simplistic invention used to discern whether objects were "electric" or "nonelectric." She glanced over at the object on top of her bookcase, comparing it to the picture in the book.

Some years ago, during her apprenticeship at Elektron, she'd constructed her own vesorium: a simple metal upright rod that rose from a flanged base to a point upon which balanced a thin arrowlike pointer of balsam. It had taken her weeks to correctly balance that piece of wood, to allow

The Electric Cupid

the metal-encased end to swing back and forth without collapsing.

And Lindsey saw, with self-satisfaction, that her replica now pointed in the direction of her stereo.

The digital clock flashed at her: 12:24. Lindsey sighed. The fluorescent lighting job at the Children's Museum yesterday had only given her four and half hours' work. And today wasn't going to be any more strenuous: a six-hour job at the most. And to top it off, the homeowner had requested she not arrive until one o'clock.

Lindsey wondered how Harry had managed to finagle that one with the local power plant. Normally, they were pretty finicky about overtime. The client, Lindsey surmised, must either be of some prestige—or a friend.

"Give me something to fill up the morning at least, Harry," she'd pleaded.

"Believe me, McGinty, I've got more paperwork than jobs this week." He'd folded his big red hands behind his balding head, and regarded one of his best employees with a soporific expression, his exasperation evident in his slow exhalation. "I don't understand you, McGinty. You've accumulated almost three times as much vacation time as any one of my employees . . ."

But Lindsey wasn't interested in a vacation. Where would she go? What would she do? Her parents were living now in Florida, but lazing on the beach and loping around with retired people didn't exactly arouse her interest.

And her two brothers, both working as attorneys in Los Angeles, were busy with their own families. She'd only be in the way.

Of course, there was Rhonda's invitation to accompany her and Rick to Hawaii. However, as nice as that sounded, Lindsey did not relish crashing her best friend's first real romantic trip with her husband. Least of all did she want to feel like some charity case, having Rhonda spend all her time attempting to fill her social calendar, as Lindsey knew her friend would.

No, she would much prefer to stay right here in Boston and work. And it wasn't as if work didn't fill a need in her. Indeed, her work left her with a tremendous feeling of satisfaction, a feeling of accomplishment; for Lindsey truly did love her job at Elektron.

She enjoyed the complexity of the electrical wires, being able to manipulate and harness that elusive power of electricity. And every assignment, it seemed, was different—an entirely new adventure in itself—even when she was sent to do something she'd done a hundred times before. Like installing a new electrical panel.

She jerked herself out of her reflections, and glanced over at the digital clock. With a yawn, she rose from the couch and stretched. The movement sent a small darting pain across the back of her jaw, a jarring reminder of the condition of her yet-to-be-pulled wisdom tooth. She groaned inwardly as she buttoned up her coveralls and shoved her feet into her work boots. Opening her toolbox, she cursorily surveyed its contents with a satisfied nod: everything tucked into its neat little compartment. The precut #3 wire and PVC pipe sat waiting for her at the door, and earlier this morning she'd loaded the truck with the drywall and plywood for the new panel. As long as they arrived at the appointed time to turn off the power, Lindsey was ready.

Lindsey glanced down at the clipboard work order again as she turned left on St. James Avenue, rounded it, then took another left on Perry Road. House number 3, 5, 7 . . .

Lindsey drew up along the shoulder of the driveway, observing the telltale signs of the pulled meter base and stray wire in the driveway. Good, they had already been there.

Parked on the other side was a milky brown Chevrolet,

an older model, antiquated but in relatively good condition. However, in this affluent Cambridge neighborhood, the car's flaws and scars advertised themselves like conspicuous smudges marring an immaculate white background.

Although Lindsey found it odd someone choosing to live in this area would drive an obviously secondhand vehicle, she could not help but smile faintly. She was remembering a time when she herself had been the owner of one daisy-yellow Volkswagen Bug, a $125 purchase that ultimately cost her five times that, as it broke down an average of three times a week.

Lindsey grinned with the memory, gathering up her equipment and tools, passing a quick glance over the worksheet again. But her grin suddenly faded as her eyes stopped short, blinking in disbelief as she took in the name scribbled at the top:

Max Rupert.

Her heart gave an involuntary squeeze, and she touched her cheek. Could it be—?

The owner of the house opened the front door as she started up the pathway.

"Hello! You're right on time! The utility company was just here—"

Lindsey looked up, and the man's mouth gaped slightly in surprise. But almost immediately his face broke into a wide grin.

"Well, well! This is a coincidence! Lindsey McGinty, how nice to see you again."

Lindsey smiled, her lips quivering a little. A jolt of adrenaline zipped through her body, and she could feel the beginnings of a blush flaming her cheeks. She compressed her lips, furrowing her brow in frustration.

"I see the swelling has already gone down," he observed, grinning. The sun glinted off his face, bringing out the natural glow in his cheeks. The eyes that continued to study Lindsey were cheerful and sober at the same time, the tiny gold flecks amid the sea of hazel-brown shining like dapples of sunlight.

"Here," he said, reaching for her toolbox, "let me help you."

"No, that's all right, Dr. Rupert. I can manage, thank you."

"Max—please, call me Max. After all, I am your . . . dentist." The corners of his eyes crinkled in amusement, and the cleft in his chin grew more pronounced. He continued to stand there, blocking the doorway, watching her with his head inclined slightly to the side.

Lindsey chewed on her lip. "Er, I could try working here on your doorstep, but it might be a little difficult."

"Oh, yes. Of course." He stepped inside.

"Unless, you'd, er, like me to come in the back way?" She glanced down at her work boots. "I don't want to mess—"

"No, no. Come on in. Believe me, there's nothing to mess up in here." He summoned her inside.

He'd spoken the truth; for as Lindsey stepped inside she was immediately struck by the nakedness of the vestibule. She took in the bare white walls of the adjoining room, noting the total absence of any knicknacks or furniture. She glanced over at the stacks of boxes shoved against the walls, all the while listening to the echoing *clomp! clomp! clomp!* of her boots against the hardwood floors.

"As you can see, I'm still in the process of moving in." He shot her a sheepish smile. "I have been for a couple of months now. I never did learn the art of decorating. But that's what I get for living in a house full of sisters." He laughed.

"I grew up with two brothers," said Lindsey.

"I guess you had your work cut out for you, then."

Lindsey's brow shot up, and she glanced at him sharply. "Yes, all women are natural decorators. I think it must be

The Electric Cupid

genetic or something,'' she said, not bothering to disguise her sarcasm.

"Oh, I didn't mean—"

"Maybe you'd better show me to the basement."

Max scratched his head, looking vaguely uncomfortable. "Uh, yes. Of course."

He led her through the kitchen, past a round maple wood table seated by four mismatched chairs, the only evidence of furniture Lindsey had observed thus far.

Lindsey frowned: His house and his life were *his* business. *You're just the electrician,* she reminded herself, shifting the wire on her shoulder, her fingers tightening around the handle of her toolbox as they descended the narrow stairway.

"The guys from the utility company said they'd be back around seven," he said behind her. "I hope I didn't mess up your schedule."

"You're paying for their overtime." Lindsey shrugged, setting down her toolbox next to the old panel. As she turned, she bumped up against him. She shivered, the hair on her forearms suddenly standing on end.

"I guess I'd better get out of your way," said Max, grinning apologetically.

"I just have to get a few more things from the truck," she said, moving past him. Again, as her arm brushed up against him, she felt that odd tingling sensation course through her body, a startling feeling much like the first time she'd mistakenly shocked herself clamping two live wires together.

What is wrong with you, Lindsey? She rubbed her arm.

He followed her up the stairs. "Let me help you."

She swiveled around at the top of the stairs, and gave him a brief smile. "Thanks, but I've got everything under control."

Max exhaled and his lips tightened into a thin line. "It's a wise woman—uh, *person*—who accepts help when it is offered." Beneath the cheeriness of his words was an undertone of command, suggesting to Lindsey that he was not a man used to having his instructions countermanded.

He followed her out to her truck, and helped her slide out the sheet of drywall from her cab.

"I can take this, if it's too heavy for you," she said.

Max beat his chest with his fists and intoned mockingly: "Me big strong man. Me can carry anything; me have big muscles." He flexed his arms and growled.

Lindsey eyed him uncertainly. "It's just that I'm used to all this lifting," she said.

"And I'm just a measly ol' dentist, is that it? You think dentists are weaklings?"

"No, of course not—"

He hefted the drywall, staggering a little, his face purpling slightly. "See? I—" He grunted. "—got it."

Lindsey watched him stumble up the pathway, feeling a slow grin creep across her face. She shut the back of her cab and picked up the lightweight slab of plywood, and hurried after him.

Max rested at the top of the basement stairs, leaning the drywall against the wall.

"Need any help?"

"No," he said, a little breathlessly. "I can manage."

Lindsey grinned. "Well, you know what they say: 'It's a wise person who accepts help when—' "

"Okay, okay," Max relented. "You take the other end."

When they'd finally managed to get the sheet of drywall down the stairs without damaging it, Max mopped his brow. "Too bad they didn't have a drywall carrying race at the Electricians' Fair. I think I would've won hands down."

Lindsey chuckled silently. It would've been much easier if she'd just carried it down herself.

"You and I—we make a good team, don't you think?"

He stared at the old electrical panel, squinting one eye, then the other. "So where do we begin?"

"We?" Lindsey compressed her lips. "Rewiring a panel isn't exactly, er, the same as drilling holes in teeth," said Lindsey.

"There you go again—making fun of my profession."

"Well, a dentist is a little different than an electrician," Lindsey pointed out.

Max turned his hazel-brown eyes on her, his gaze lingering for a moment, a thoughtfulness drawing his strong features together.

Lindsey opened her toolbox, trying to quash her sudden self-consciousness and concentrate on the job at hand. She could feel his eyes intent on her, watching her, and she wished he would leave her to her task. His presence made her all the more aware of her own self, which was thrumming, humming, exuding energy like an electrified fence.

"So, Lindsey, you do much fishing around here?"

"Fishing?" Lindsey swung her head around in bemusement.

"A patient of mine was telling me about a place—where was it? Stony Pond? Stony Lake?"

"Stony Brook," she corrected. "You mean the Stony Brook River. But I've never actually fished before."

"Then I'll have to take you out there sometime." He grinned. "I think you'll like fishing. It'll help you relax."

Lindsey inclined her head slightly, casting him a brief sidelong glance before she began ripping out the panel. "Are you implying that I don't relax?"

"Well, you do seem a little tense." His tone was light, mocking, almost as if he were testing her, curious to see what kind of reaction he could arouse from her. "Or is it just me?"

"Excuse me?" Lindsey inspected the old breaker she pulled from the panel. Max moved closer. The pulse in her neck drummed a rapid bongo beat as she caught a whiff of his spicy, musky scent. She feigned deep interest in the breaker, though it was but an ordinary 60 amp, and essentially now a useless piece of equipment.

"Do I make you nervous?" asked Max.

"No, of course not," Lindsey quipped, perhaps a little too quickly. Despite the coolness of the basement, beads of sweat were beginning to gather conspiratorially at the small of her back and the base of her throat.

"Good. How about this weekend, then? Say, Saturday?"

Lindsey frowned at him. "You mean—go fishing?"

"Don't tell me you're not up to new experiences. You strike me as a woman of adventure." He flashed her a smile, a challenging glint in his eyes. "Or is it that you think fishing is only a man's sport?"

Lindsey's back went rigid, her eyes suddenly narrowing.

"Okay, then," Max nodded, reading acceptance of his invitation in her expression. "Saturday it is. I'll pick you up—"

"I-I can't. Not this Saturday."

"Oh. Then how about Sunday?" But then Max winced, suddenly remembering a previous appointment. "No, Sunday's not good for me. How about next—"

"Hello! Max? Hello-o-o!"

Lindsey and Max swiveled their gaze to the top of the stairs. A woman poked her head around the banister. She started down the stairs.

"Oh, here you are! What are you doing down—" The woman stopped short when she saw Lindsey.

Lindsey stared back at the woman, immediately recognizing Charlene Waters.

"Hey, Charlene!" greeted Max. He turned to Lindsey. "You already know Lindsey."

"Yes," said Charlene, her smile saccharin sweet. "Hello, again, Mrs. McGinty."

That's Miss *McGinty,* Lindsey amended silently. "Hello." She waved a screwdriver at her.

"You do seem to pop up at the most unlikely times," said Charlene, pursing together her pink lipsticked lips.

"Lindsey's doing some electrical work for me," said Max.

From his cheerful tone, Lindsey gauged he hadn't sensed the sudden change in the air. However, Lindsey could feel the cloud of tension break over her head and swarm about them like a suffocating blanket. Her skin prickled as Charlene's catlike eyes sized her up, and she had a vision of the woman's talons springing forth as she prepared to pounce.

But Charlene only leaned back on the banister, her mouth turning up into a cool smile. "Oh, how interesting. You're a construction worker, Mrs. McGinty."

This time Lindsey did not hesitate to correct her. "It's *Miss* McGinty. And I'm not a construction worker; I'm an electrician."

"Oh, yes, well." Charlene shrugged, not bothering to veil the condescension in her voice. She smiled brightly at Max. "Max? I've come to play your humble maid." She curtsied prettily, displaying her spandex lavender track suit that accentuated the round curves of her slender build. As she laughed, she tossed back her long strawberry blond hair. "See? I've even dressed for the occasion."

"You're an angel, Charlene," said Max, starting for the stairs.

"Well, this place could use a woman's touch." Charlene giggled.

Max turned to Lindsey. "You're okay? You don't need anything?"

"Let her do her job, Maxy. After all, that's what you're paying her for," said Charlene, reaching forward to clasp his hand. "As for me, I'm here of my own free will. Not to say that I won't extract some kind of payment later." She winked at him mischievously.

"Uh-oh." Max's face assumed a mock look of terror.

"You're not going to make me take you out to another one of those posh restaurants, are you? That last meal actually cost more than my car."

Charlene sniffed and rolled her eyes. "Tightwad," she teased, but her gaze flickered to Lindsey, and a sudden smugness crept into her expression.

Lindsey watched them clamber up the stairs. As she proceeded to disassemble the old panel, she heard Charlene giggling upstair. Max let out a loud guffaw. Their footsteps echoed from upstairs; shuffling noises of boxes being dragged across the floor and snatches of conversation drifted down to Lindsey's ears:

". . . oooh! remember this, Max?"

A muffled response.

". . . can't believe you still have that old thing! Max, I gave that to you on your eighteenth birthday. . . . Look at us! We were so young then! . . . You look so handsome, Max. . . . And what's this? Ooooh! . . ."

Lindsey winced at Charlene's squeal of delight and forced all her attention back to the panel. After a moment, however, she could feel the muscles in her jaw tightening. Small darts of pain shot across the left side of her face, and she realized then she was clenching her teeth together.

She rubbed at the tautness in her neck and flexed her shoulders. At the same time she was aware of a strange sourness roiling inside her stomach. As she pressed her hand to her belly, Charlene's abrupt shriek of laughter upstairs jarred her, making her react with a scowl. She grumbled under her breath.

Why was she so agitated all of a sudden? Normally, her level of concentration was such that even a large group of drunken tourists couldn't distract her from her work.

Lindsey took in a deep breath and stared at the panel. In her head she rehearsed the job, a procedure she'd performed at least a hundred times before: Run new piping, replace the 60 amps with 200s, pull wire down the stack, tie to meter base . . .

Lindsey smiled, suddenly feeling her old enthusiasm come flooding back. Twirling the screwdriver between her fingers like a professional gunslinger, she eyed her opponent and attacked, delving into her task with a willful smile on her lips, whistling an old Civil War marching tune between her teeth.

"Hello," said a voice from the bottom of the stairs.

Lindsey whirled around, startled.

Charlene gazed back at her, disciplined composure stretching her delicate features into a relaxed smile. But as she held the glass of water out to Lindsey, the smile thinned noticeably. "Thought you could use a drink. Unfortunately this is all we have right now; we haven't done any serious grocery shopping yet."

We? "Thanks." Lindsey took it, and cast the woman a tentative smile. She noted the contrast in their skin tones, with Charlene's well-manicured, creamy hand making hers appear more dirty and ruddy than they actually were.

"I hope we haven't been distracting you." But there was no trace of apology in Charlene's voice. "Max and I have just been reminiscing about the good ol' days," she said, smiling wistfully.

"You see," she went on, enunciating each word slowly, carefully, "we've known each other since high school. Max and I, we're very close—well, you understand how it is . . . childhood sweethearts, and all that."

Lindsey nodded. *So,* she thought, *Charlene and Max were high school sweethearts.* Her stomach suddenly cramped up; her chest ached, and she fought to keep the smile on her face.

An uncomfortable silence elapsed between them, and Lindsey's facial muscles tightened with the strain of her smile. The longer she stood in this petite porcelainlike woman's presence, the more awkward and clumsy Lindsey began to feel. And yet, it was becoming clearer to Lindsey, as Charlene stood facing her, that this woman, despite her refined delicateness, was not a woman without defenses.

Indeed the fierceness in Charlene's eyes, the way she held herself, with arms folded across her chest, her chin thrust slightly forward—it all served to convey a supreme self-confidence, if not a signal to warn all those who might dare to confront her. And Lindsey guessed that when provoked, this woman could easily defeat any who trespassed into her territory, who threatened her—

But I'm not a threat to her, mused Lindsey silently, confused by her own train of thought. Could she be mistaken in sensing these feelings from this woman? This guardedness, the suspicion Lindsey'd glimpsed in her catlike eyes? Was she somehow misinterpreting Charlene's signals?

"How's the tooth?" asked Charlene, breaking into her thoughts. "I see the swelling is gone."

"Yes. The, er, antibiotics appear to be helping," said Lindsey, returning Charlene's smile. *Yes,* she thought, *I have misjudged this woman.*

"It's all quite a coincidence, isn't it?"

That aura of territoriality drifted back, settling between them like some ominous mist. Lindsey frowned slightly, pushing her way through the mushrooming tension. "Excuse me?"

Charlene's smile did not waver, but her eyes seemed to lengthen and darken in the basement light. "Well, it seems rather odd, don't you think? One day you're becoming a patient of Max's—and then out of the blue you suddenly show up here to work on his house."

Max had said the same thing, only the implication in Charlene's tone was somehow different. "Yes, it is a coincidence," agreed Lindsey, not certain why the hairs at the back of her neck were beginning to rise.

The green eyes sharpened and continued to gaze at her.

Charlene's face was very still as she spoke: "Me, I don't believe in coincidences. From my experience, there's usually someone—" She moistened her lips. "—someone behind it all, someone who plans very carefully—"

"You two getting acquainted down there?" Max tromped down the stairs and poked his head around the banister. "Anybody up for some Indian food? I was thinking of ordering in some dinner."

Charlene looked up at him. "Now, you just wait a minute, Dr. Max Rupert. I thought we agreed you were going to take *me* out on the town."

Max gazed at Lindsey. "Well, I thought Lindsey might—"

Lindsey glanced at her watch. "Actually, those guys should be here soon, and I'm just about done."

"Great! You like Indian food?" Max grinned, oblivious to Charlene's signaling look. But Lindsey did not fail to notice it.

"Er, I don't want to—" Her eyes met Charlene's, and for an instant Lindsey could feel that old competitive spirit rise within her and rear its familiar head. *You are not in competition with this woman,* she told herself. *There is nothing for you to compete for.* Lindsey glanced at Max. His eyes studied her back. Immediately she shifted her gaze back to Charlene, cringing inwardly as her neck and face grew warm.

"Actually, I already have plans for tonight," she told them. And this wasn't exactly a lie; Lenny'd asked her a couple of days ago to come down to his place and take a look at the hall light. "But, er, thanks for the invitation." She returned her attention to the panel.

Charlene climbed the stairs, her hand moving to encircle Max's waist. "It looks like it's just you and me, Maxy. Just like old times," she purred. "Why don't you make reservations for us at that place Mrs. Honeysuckle was talking about—the Coach Bistro, wasn't it?"

Lindsey lifted her brows. The Coach Bistro was one of Boston's most elite restaurants.

"Well—" Max hesitated.

"Oh, come on, Maxy." Charlene twisted her long, slender arms about his shoulders, trapping him. "We've been working all afternoon. And it's not as if you're paying me to help you." Charlene emphasized the word "paying," which, Lindsey supposed, was for her—the "construction worker's"—benefit.

"Okay, okay. You've worn down my resistance. Go and get ready, and I'll pick you up—" He checked his watch. "—in about an hour?" He was looking at Lindsey as he said this.

Lindsey nodded. "I'll be out of here in half an hour," she assured him.

"No rush, Lindsey." He smiled as Charlene took his arm and led him upstairs.

Lindsey was doing her final walkabout, scrutinizing her work, when Max came down.

"Ah, looks good," said Max, standing next to her.

She could smell his aftershave, that scent of spice and musk that by now was permanently imprinted in her memory. His hair was still damp, and he'd combed it up from his high forehead. He fiddled with his tie and buttoned the cuffs of his shirt.

"Er, I've labeled the switches, as you can see." She pointed to the new panel. "These are for the kitchen; here's the refrigerator—"

"How do I look?"

Lindsey turned to gaze at him. *Like a beautiful, dashing dentist,* she answered silently. *You can brush my teeth anytime, Dr. Max Rupert.*

"You look nice. Hmmm... just a sec." She reached up—and impulsive act—and flipped down his collar, smoothing it with her fingers. As she did this her fingers brushed up against the warm damp skin of his neck, and she jerked back her hand and flushed.

His smile broadened and the hazel in his eyes darkened as he watched her. But, too, Lindsey glimpsed something almost arrogant in the way he looked at her, his amusement splayed all too plainly across his face. And Lindsey could feel herself suddenly growing rigid, irritation mounting in her.

"You have a date tonight?" he asked.

"Yes—er, I mean no." A date? With Lenny? "I'm helping . . . a friend," she added.

"Not a boyfriend?"

"No." Lindsey stepped back and banged her boot heel against the toolbox. Her other foot stumbled over the remaining coil of wire, and as her arms flailed out, windmilling, trying to regain her balance, strong hands reached out and grabbed her waist.

Max held her for a moment, their bodies barely touching. "You okay?" He gazed into her flushed face with concern. But there was still that hint of amusement in his expression; it was the look an adult might give a clumsy child. Lindsey jerked quickly out of his embrace, annoyed with him—and herself for reacting to his touch. Why was she all of a sudden tingling?

"You look a little shaken. You're not forgetting to take your amoxicillin, are you?"

Lindsey's hand went to her cheek. As if on cue, a dull ache pulsed through her jaw. "I'm perfectly capable of following instructions," she replied tartly. She was surprised by her own curtness.

"Look, if the pain is still bothering you, I have some Tylenol in the bathroom up—"

The phone rang upstairs.

"No, really. I'm fine. I-I've had worse."

"You're one tough cookie, aren't you?" His eyes crinkled a smile.

The phone continued to ring.

"Er, don't you think you'd better answer that?"

Max glanced up at the door. "You almost finished here? Would you like a drink, or something? I've got water, and . . . well, that's about it." He laughed. "I haven't had much time to do any grocery shopping."

Don't you mean "we"—you and Charlene—haven't had time to grocery shop? "Actually, I'm done here," she said, tossing her pliers into the toolbox. "You're all set. They've put in a new meter base and the power's back on. Everything seems to be in . . . working order." Her words stumbled over themselves. Why was she babbling like this? Why was she acting so nervous? Lindsey wiped her hands on her coveralls and lock-snapped the clasps on her toolbox.

"Please, allow me." And before she could stop him, he gripped the toolbox handle and hefted it. "Oooof! What do you have in here? Cement?"

Lindsey coiled the extra wire around her shoulder. "Too heavy for you?" she teased.

"I'm a dentist, not a weight lifter." He grunted, starting up the stairs awkwardly.

The phone was still ringing when they reached the top of the stairs. Max set down the toolbox in the kitchen and answered it.

"Hi . . . No, I was just helping Lindsey," he said into the receiver. "Yes, she's still here. . . . No, they just left. . . . I'll be heading out in a couple of minutes. . . . Don't worry, we'll make it in time. . . . Okay, Charlene . . . bye."

He smiled at Lindsey. "So what'll it be?" He rubbed his palms together. "How about a nice tall glass of water?"

"I should get going—"

"Well, before you do, I, uh, would like your opinion on something." He scratched his head, glancing about the kitchen.

Lindsey spied the large framed photograph on the

counter. A younger, grinning version of Max in a tuxedo stood next to a beautiful young woman wearing a pearly white evening gown: Charlene. The catlike eyes gleamed happily at the photographer, long strawberry blond tresses cascading like silk scarves across her ivory shoulders. Lindsey passed a brusque hand over her own shorn, dark hair.

Prom night, guessed Lindsey, admiring Charlene's apparently timeless beauty.

"So what do you think?"

Lindsey stared at the photograph. "High school sweethearts," she murmured.

"What was that?" Max cupped his ear, raising his brows.

Lindsey shifted her gaze from the photograph to him. "I'm sorry. I, er, was thinking about something else. What was the question?"

Max reached over and picked up the photograph, shaking his head. "If it were up to Charlene, this place would be wall-to-wall photographs." He set it back down with a sigh. "I guess she misses Saint Andrews." He smiled.

Do you miss Saint Andrews? she silently queried him, for she had glimpsed in that moment the sudden look that breezed across his features, a wistful shadow that took him away for an instant, which now made its home in the hazel-brown eyes.

"Er, you were saying?" she prompted finally.

"Oh, right." The hazel-brown eyes returned to focus on her face, then shifted to the ceiling. "Recessed lighting. I was thinking of installing two or three high-hat lights along here." He sidestepped toward the built-in cabinets and pointed to the ceiling. "The lighting over here is a little dim, don't you think?"

"High-hat lights will brighten the area, yes," said Lindsey.

"So?" Max blinked at her, waiting.

"So—er, yes. Yes. I think it's a good idea."

"And? Can you do it? Or is it too complicated for you?"

Lindsey's eyebrows twitched; the corners of her lips tightened. "No, I don't think this is beyond my capabilities," she said, meeting his gaze squarely. Why did this man insist on challenging her?

"Wonderful! When can you start?"

"I'll, er, have to talk to Harry. Contracting jobs must go through him first."

"I'll speak to Harry myself," said Max, shrugging on his jacket. "And I'll put in a good word for you while I'm at it."

"I don't need you to do that for me," said Lindsey.

His eyebrows quirked up. "Well, he did tell me he was sending me one of his best electricians—"

The phone rang, and Max picked it up. "Hello?... Harry, hello! What a coincidence! We were just talking about you." Max gave Lindsey a sideways glance. "... No, don't worry." Max laughed. "Lindsey? Yes, she's still here...." He handed her the phone and smiled. "He wants to talk to you."

"Harry?" she said into the receiver, her eyes flickering up to meet Max's. She turned around so he couldn't see the self-conscious flush staining her cheeks.

"Lindsey," greeted Harry. "Just checking to see if the power company made it there yet."

"Yeah, they left about ten minutes ago."

"Good." She heard him sigh, and visualized him rubbing the bald spot on the top of his head.

"So, is that it?" Max signaled to her that he wanted to talk to Harry. "Er, hold on, Harry. Max—Dr. Rupert wants to speak with you." She handed Max the receiver.

"Harry? I just wanted to say thanks for sending Lindsey over here. And, well, I was so impressed with her work I'd like her to do another job for me.... Yes, she is." He let out a low laugh, his gaze flitting over to Lindsey.

"... Great ... Next Wednesday? Perfect ... Uh-huh. Talk to you later, Harry ... bye." He hung up.

"So it's settled." He rubbed his hands together. "You're on the job."

"Oh," was all Lindsey could say, although her heart leaped a little in her chest at the prospect of spending another day with this man. She picked up her toolbox. "Well, I'd better be going."

Max held open the door for her. "See you Monday, Lindsey," he called after her.

She turned her head slightly and saw that he was still standing in the doorway. The early setting sun pinked the sky behind him, and the approaching dusk shadows fell across his tall figure. Lindsey watched him tilt his head up toward the sky, striking a serene, almost majestic pose. The sight of him at that moment aroused in her a curious sensation, raising the hackles at the back of her neck. At the same time her chest tightened, and a throbbing pulsed in her throat.

This vision of Max Rupert stayed with Lindsey as she turned down Garden Street, and so caught up she was in trying to unravel her peculiar reaction that she nearly bolted through the red light.

A crossing car, already starting across the intersection, honked angrily at her as she slammed the brakes. Lindsey blinked, prespiration suddenly prickling around her hairline as she was jolted out of her reverie.

She rubbed her eyes, feeling more weary than she had in a long time—but at the same time feeling, too, a kinetic kind of energy surge through her. She glanced down at her grubby hands and thought, but for a slight, strange moment, that they were glowing.

It's only a trick of the light, she dismissed with a brief shake of her head. But her heart was a fevered rush in her ears, and as she gripped the steering wheel, her hands felt as though they could melt through the plastic.

What was wrong with her? Was she ill? The light turned green, and Lindsey roared off, deliberately letting her thoughts drift away with the speed.

Chapter Four

Lindsey climbed the stepladder and scrutinized Lenny's hall light. She prodded the circuitry, then stepped down.

"Can you fix it?" asked Lenny, smoothing back his wiry cowlick.

Lindsey nodded, her eyes stinging from the too-strong smell of cologne that pervaded the basement apartment. She held her breath as she moved past him to rummage inside her toolbox. After a moment her fingers closed on an unused light bulb. She climbed back up the stepladder, unscrewed the old light bulb, and inserted the new one.

"Try it now," she instructed.

Lenny flicked the switch and the hall lit up.

"Gee," said Lenny with a sheepish smile.

Lindsey gave him a sidelong glance. "Anything else?"

"Well." Lenny hitched up his jeans. "Since you're already here, you might as well stay for dinner," he said with a leering grin. "I could rustle us up some chow—you like chili? I got some left over in the fridge—"

"You owe me seventy cents for the light bulb," said Lindsey, folding up the stepladder.

"Why don't I just buy you dinner?" he suggested, blocking her way. "Aw, come on, Lindsey. You gotta eat. And I've got these two-for-one coupons for Burger Knight that are just taking up space on my fridge door."

Lindsey hesitated. She *was* hungry, she thought, and her stomach confirmed this with a low growl. Upstairs, she only had a couple of slices of bread and some freezer-burnt hot dogs to choose from.

"Yeah, okay. Why not?" She shrugged.

"Really?" said Lenny, taken aback. But his surprise quickly fled from his face, replaced by a sudden smug look of confidence. He sniffed loudly, and ran his hands through his cowlick again, grinning. "We'll take my car. Just got it souped up the other day."

Lindsey, too tired and hungry to argue, conceded with a sigh.

Lenny hurried to the door and opened it for her, his face beaming like an eager puppy dog's.

"Man, you *were* hungry," said Lenny, swerving his Camaro around a rapidly moving Lamborghini. "I don't think I've ever seen a woman wolf down two burgers that fast."

Lindsey grimaced. The truth was, Lindsey didn't want anyone she knew to catch her there with Lenny. On the way over to Burger Knight she'd thought she'd made it clear to her downstairs neighbor that they were *not* on an official date. Nonetheless, Lenny had persisted in making overt remarks to the counter girl, infuriating Lindsey as he referred to her as "my ol' lady" and "my main squeeze."

"Well, we still got some time to kill. I can slip in a video. You like kung fu movies?" He sped up, the roar of his engine grating in their ears as he paced a speeding Porsche.

Lindsey grasped the strap of her seat belt and pressed her foot down on an imaginary break. "Er, Lenny? Don't you think you'd better slow down a bit?" Grimacing, she clenched her teeth together as the Porsche honked angrily at them.

"Hey, this ol' girl can outrun anything on the road. Worked over her engine myself—" An ominous *kerclunk! clunk!* sounded from the front end of the car as the Camaro suddenly jerked forward. The dashboard beneath Lindsey's fingers began to vibrate.

"Er, maybe we'd better pull over, Lenny."

They were slowing now, and Lenny pounded the dash. "No, it's all right. She'll pick up." He shifted gears as cars sped past.

"Lenny." Lindsey glanced behind them in frustration. They puttered along the middle lane, the car sputtering and clanking in protest. "Pull over," she ordered.

Lenny broke clear of the traffic, and sidled along the shoulder of the highway. The Camaro uttered a final resigned sigh and gave up. Lenny tried the ignition. It wheezed and died. He glanced over at Lindsey, wincing an embarrassed smile, and tried again. The car whinnied a little and then shuddered into silence.

"Just give me a minute. She does this once in a while," he muttered. "Could you—?" He motioned to the glove compartment.

Lindsey flipped open the glove compartment and pressed the button to pop the hood.

"She's just a little temperamental sometimes," he assured her, opening his door.

"You need any help?" Lindsey massaged her neck wearily.

"Nah. This won't take long."

Ten minutes passed, and Lindsey got out, groaning under her breath. This was her own fault; after all, how many times had she seen this car being towed from their driveway? How many mornings had she had to give Lenny a ride to work?

Lenny was shining the flashlight at the engine, shaking his head in bewilderment. "I can't figure out what's wrong with her."

Lindsey peered under the hood. "Hmmm... looks like the alternator might be shot—and that carburetor doesn't look too healthy." In fact, it looked to her as if the car needed an entirely new engine. She eyed the balding tires and the loose, rusted bumper. The body was almost in better shape than the interior.

"Maybe it's time you thought about investing in a new car, Lenny."

Lenny wiped his nose with the back of his hand. "She's still got some life in her," he said, a little forlornly.

Car lights slowed and slid behind them. Lindsey glanced around the hood to see a man climb out.

"Need any help?" he shouted, waving. As he began to approach, the passenger—a woman—stepped out and beckoned to him.

The man ignored her and came around to where Lenny and Lindsey stood. "Hi. You folks in trouble?"

Lindsey's heart performed a sudden skip jump as the light reflected off the man's face.

"Well, hello, Lindsey?" Max Rupert smiled at her, surprised.

Of all the people to run into—

Lenny swiveled his gaze from Max to Lindsey, then back to Max. "You know this guy, Lindsey?" His eyes narrowed suspiciously.

"In a manner of speaking." Max grinned.

Warmth seeped into Lindsey's face, and her fingers moved automatically to her left cheek. "Er, yes. This is my . . . dentist," she said.

"And Lindsey here, is my electrician," said Max. The intensity of his gaze made her flush, and she glanced down at the engine, hoping neither of these men could sense her sudden nervousness.

"Max Rupert," Max introduced himself.

"Lenny Bryce." They shook hands, and Max peered under the hood.

"We think it might be the alternator or the carburetor," said Lenny, hitching up his jeans.

"Hmmm . . . you could be right. Listen, I've got a cellular phone in the car. I can call a tow truck for you," said Max.

"Hey, thanks." Lenny slammed down the hood.

They strode back to Max's car where the woman stood, waiting, with arms folded across her chest. Lindsey immediately recognized that porcelain skin that seemed to glow ghostly pale in the moonlight: Charlene.

"We can give you a lift as soon as the tow truck gets here," said Max, glancing at Lindsey. "Where're you two headed?"

"My place," said Lenny before Lindsey could respond.

"Oh, you two are—"

"Max, is everything all—" Charlene's words faltered as her eyes fell on Lindsey. "Oh, Miss McGinty." Her voice dropped noticeably in temperature. "Fancy meeting you here." But her gaze moved directly to Lenny who was staring at her, his mouth gaping slightly.

"Hello." She smiled. "You must be Miss McGinty's boyfriend."

"Lenny, this is Charlene Waters," Max introduced.

Lenny's fingers smoothed back his wiry cowlick before he clasped her outstretched hand in both of his. "A pleasure to meet you, Charlene."

Charlene's small, pert nose wrinkled as she smiled back at him, looking as though she'd just tasted something unsavory. "Yes," she said, extracting her hand from his.

"Charlene. That's a beautiful name," intoned Lenny. "I had an Aunt Charlene once. She owned a chicken farm in Iowa—"

"Yes, well," Charlene interrupted him with a dismissive smile. "It was certainly nice meeting you, Lenny—" She nodded to Lindsey and smiled at Max. "Max, honey? Shouldn't we be on our way now?"

"Their car won't start. I'm going to call a tow truck," said Max, reaching inside for his cellular phone. "If you want, we can wait with you until it gets here," he suggested to Lenny.

"It's getting late, Max."

Max glanced over at Lindsey. "Well, why don't you take the Chevy to your place—you could drop Lindsey off on your way."

Lenny glanced at Lindsey. "Yeah, that's a good idea."

"Do the women get a say in this?" muttered Lindsey.

"Hey, you cold? You're shivering," Lenny put his arm around her.

Lindsey shot him a warning look, and Lenny dropped his arm with a rueful smile.

"Here, you want my jacket, Lindsey?" Max started to take off his suit jacket.

"No, no. I'm fine." She pursed her lips, struggling to suppress her mounting irritation.

"Well, *I'm* a little chilled," said Charlene, moving to Max, and snuggling close to him.

"Yes, the evening has cooled down quite a bit, hasn't it?" said Max, staring up at the star-studded sky. "Hmmm ... no sense you waiting out here, too. I don't know how long it'll take the tow truck to get here. Charlene, why don't you take the Chevy? Lenny and Lindsey and I'll grab a taxi—"

"I can drive Lindsey home," suggested Charlene quickly.

Max glanced at Lindsey. "Is that okay with you? We don't want to mess up your plans."

Mess up what plans? thought Lindsey. She sighed resignedly. "No, that'd be great," she said, moving to the passenger side of the Chevy.

Charlene kissed Max's cheek and gestured to Lenny. "Don't you worry. I'll get her home in one piece," she assured him with a smile.

Lenny started toward Lindsey, but she'd already climbed

into the Chevy and she pulled the door shut with a brusque wave.

As they drove off, Lindsey glanced back at the two silhouetted figures leaning against the Camaro: Lenny, round-shouldered and puppy-doglike in his stance; Max, a tall and masterly apparition impressing itself even against the summer evening shadows.

"So," Charlene interrupted her thoughts. "Lenny seems . . . nice."

"Yes."

"Is Lenny an electrician, too?"

"No, he's a mason."

"Hmmm . . . yes. That makes sense." Charlene nodded. "How long have you two been seeing each other?"

Lindsey stifled a laugh. "Oh, Lenny and I aren't together. He's my neigh—"

"You'll have to direct me to your house," Charlene cut in.

"You'll be turning right up here on Globe Street."

Charlene shook her head. "I don't know if I would ever get used to living in such a big city," she said. "Max and I—we're small-town people at heart. Granted, there's so much to see in this city, but we can't help but feel a little homesick for Saint Andrews. You ever been to New Brunswick, Lindsey?"

"No. Though I hear it's quite beautiful."

"Oh, you probably wouldn't like our little town. Saint Andrews is nothing like Boston. Funny, though, in a city this size, with all these people, you'd never think of running into someone you know." She glanced over at Lindsey, a hint of a smile on her lips. "Another coincidence." She laughed.

But there was no warmth in that laugh, and Lindsey thought she heard a twinge of suspicion in Charlene's tone. Surely this woman didn't suspect she'd somehow arranged for Lenny's car to break down, and for Max to come to their rescue?

"I have a feeling Max and I won't be staying here in Boston long," Charlene went on. "Max and I are a lot alike that way—we prefer the atmosphere of a small town. And, well, our families are in Saint Andrews—oh, I'm sure you understand."

That cloying aura of territoriality hovered over them, its claws reaching for Lindsey, smothering her. She rolled down the window and breathed in the night air.

"Max and I have been together since we were kids. I was a little reluctant to come to Boston, but he practically begged me. And what could I do? He'd never survive this place without me. He and I are—"

"It's your next left," said Lindsey, pulling at the neck of her T-shirt. Suddenly she was feeling very claustrophobic.

Charlene left Globe Street and nosed the Chevrolet down Langley Street. The Chevrolet jerked and rattled. Charlene exhaled a sigh of irritation. "I don't know why he bought this old thing. I've been trying to get him to drive my new Taurus, but, well . . ." She shook her head, shifting in the seat.

"Oh, what an . . . interesting neighborhood." She gazed out at the small brick and metal-sided houses, taking in the dilapidated fences, the overgrown lawns.

Lindsey was at once glad to see that Lenny'd cut the front grass, that his construction equipment was, for once, safely stored away in the garage and not spewed along the walkway.

"Well, this is it," said Lindsey, opening the passenger door.

"Maybe you and Lenny and Max and I could go out on a double date sometime," suggested Charlene, gazing at the bungalow.

"Lenny and I are just friends," said Lindsey.

The Electric Cupid

Charlene's delicate brows rose, a momentary crease appearing at the bridge of her nose. And then she smiled, almost solicitously. "That's not the impression I got from Lenny."

"Believe me," said Lindsey firmly, "there is nothing between Lenny and I."

"Oh, give it time," mused Charlene, a private utterance spoken aloud not to Lindsey, but to herself. "You'd be surprised what can happen with a little persistence."

Lindsey strode up the front walkway and let herself in. As she turned to wave at the Chevrolet and closed the door behind her, she could not help but feel a little disturbed by her conversation with Charlene.

It was obvious to Lindsey the woman didn't like her. She had gathered this much in her tone: the condescending way Charlene had spoken to her, the underlying threat Lindsey had sensed in her words. "Back off," they clearly warned.

But "back off" from what? From whom?

However, Lindsey had already guessed the answer: Charlene wanted her to stay clear of Max Rupert.

"So, what do you think?" Rhonda twirled around before the mirror. "It doesn't make me look too fat, does it?"

"No, it looks great," said Lindsey distractedly, pulling closed the plunging neckline of the dress she was trying on.

Rhonda fingered her long dangling earrings and gazed at her friend with a wistful sigh. "Wow, Lindsey. I wish I had your figure. Me? I'd look like a blimp in that dress." She gave a low whistle. "You should wear more clothes like that. Talk about gorgeous!"

Lindsey grimaced at her reflection, and shook her head. "Hmm . . . this dress, it's not me—"

"Oh, I wouldn't say that," a voice interrupted her.

Rhonda and Lindsey glanced over at the owner of the voice who stepped out from behind a rack of blouses.

"You look great," said Max with a wolfish grin.

Lindsey blushed.

Rhonda nodded. "See? Now you've got two assenting opinions. You're going to have to buy it now." She ignored her friend's warning stare, and smiled at Max. "Excuse me, have we met somewhere?" And before Max could respond, she held out her hand. "Hi, I'm Rhonda Tierney." She gestured to Lindsey. "And this is—"

"Lindsey McGinty." Max nodded, shaking Rhonda's hand. "Max Rupert," he introduced himself. "I'm . . ." He flashed Lindsey a covert look, which caused Lindsey's face to redden all the more. "I'm Lindsey's . . . dentist."

"Oh." Sudden understanding lit Rhonda's face.

Lindsey wanted to kick her.

"If you don't buy that dress, I will," said Max, seeming to enjoy Lindsey's sudden discomfort.

"Oh, you wear dresses, do you?" quipped Lindsey, her gaze moving defiantly to meet his. She prayed he couldn't hear the tympanous beat of her heart, which seemed about ready to burst through the clinging material of the dress.

Max's smile was wry. "Actually, I prefer pants."

"So do I," retorted Lindsey.

"I don't doubt it."

"What's that supposed to mean? You don't think women should wear pants?"

Max grinned broadly. "On the contrary. When women look as good as you do in pants, I'm all for it."

"But that dress does look fabulous on you, Lindsey," said Rhonda, watching them with interest.

"Yes, it does," agreed Charlene, who suddenly appeared behind Max.

She was wearing a long black evening gown, the silky material clinging to the slim curves of her petite body. As she moved seductively before Max, the slit up the side revealed a creamy, shapely leg. She ran her fingers down her porcelain throat.

"What do you think?" she asked him, fluttering her eyelashes. "Not too much, is it?"

Max gazed at her appraisingly. "Maybe a little," he said. "These convention things do tend toward the conservative."

"I think you look beautiful," said Rhonda.

Charlene flickered her green eyes in Rhonda's direction, as if noticing her for the first time. "Why, thank you, dear." She twirled around gracefully. "Well, Maxy? Should I get it?"

Max shrugged. "It's up to you. But on what I pay you, I'm not sure you can afford—"

"It'll be an early birthday present, then."

"Early, indeed. You just had your birth—"

"Oh, please, Maxy." She pressed her cheek to his arm, purring up at him like an affection-starved kitten.

Max sighed, half-groaning. "Yeah, yeah. Okay."

"You're wonderful." She planted a wet kiss on his cheek, hanging onto his arm possessively.

Lindsey noticed her triumphant green eyes swivel in her direction. With a swift sweeping gaze she took in Lindsey's attire, her slightly mocking expression making Lindsey feel all the more ridiculous and self-conscious.

"Excuse me," muttered Lindsey, quickly disappearing back into the safety of the changing room.

As she shrugged out of the dress, she heard Rhonda saying good-bye to Max and Charlene.

"Remind Lindsey we've got an appointment on Monday," Lindsey heard Max tell her. "Nine o'clock!" he added loudly, knowing she was listening.

After a moment, Rhonda knocked on the door. "You can come out now. They're gone."

Lindsey zipped up her jean shorts and slipped her feet into her sneakers. She pushed open the change room door.

"Well, that was some tennis match," said Rhonda.

"Huh?"

"You and your . . . dentist; he kept serving the ball and you kept hitting it back to him." Rhonda gave her friend a teasing grin. "A bit hard, I might add."

"Rhonda, as per usual your analogies simply boggle the mind," said Lindsey, annoyed. But her tone was lighthearted, and she could not help but smile. What was this she was feeling? Pleasure? Excitement?

"You're right about her, though. That woman doesn't like you. But—" Rhonda gazed at her reflection critically. "But I think you're wrong about them being romantically involved."

Lindsey shrugged. "It's none of my business." However, she was still feeling a leftover buzz of excitement from her and Max's "tennis match." And she paused deliberately, hoping Rhonda would qualify this last statement about Max and Charlene.

"You said they were high-school sweethearts. But it looks to me like he's got his eye on you, Lindsey—and Charlene knows it."

"That doesn't mean he's not involved with her, Rhonda." *It just means he's a flirt,* thought Lindsey. But was that what he'd been doing? Flirting with her?

"Well, he asked you out, didn't he?"

"He's new in Boston. He-he probably doesn't know many people," said Lindsey.

Rhonda gazed at her friend, a knowing glint gleaming in her gray eyes. "Well, why don't you just ask him out? See what he says?"

"Why would I do that?" Lindsey's face reddened.

Rhonda linked her arm in hers and sighed. "Because you like him."

Lindsey didn't say anything for a moment. It was true she felt strange when Max was around, and more annoyingly, her thoughts these past couple of days seemed to be full of him when he *wasn't* around. Admittedly, for some reason she found herself drawn to him; *like two polar opposites of a magnet,* she mused.

But even before she could pause to consider this idea, Lindsey compressed her lips and forcibly pushed away this thought.

"Max is just . . . my dentist," she said firmly.

Rhonda raised an eyebrow. "Just because something's invisible, doesn't mean the effects aren't real."

"What's that supposed to mean?"

"You tell me. You're the electricity expert." Rhonda returned her gaze to the mirror. "So what do you think? Huh, the floral pattern is a little loud. Maybe with a different pair of earrings—" She spied Lindsey's quick nervous glance behind her.

"They've already left," she assured her friend.

"Who?" said Lindsey innocently.

Rhonda rolled her eyes. "Don't worry. You'll see him tomorrow."

Lindsey touched her cheek, wincing slightly. But the sudden fluttering percolating in her stomach, she realized, held more excitement than anxiety.

Chapter Five

Lindsey glanced in the rearview mirror and fluffed up her short pixie-cut hair, rearranging her wisped bangs. She reached in her purse and applied pale pink lipstick to her full lips, and smiled at herself. She groaned, and with a brisk motion wiped off the lipstick.

What was she doing? She was getting a tooth pulled, not going on a date. For an instant she thought about removing her mascara as well, but she knew she'd make more of a mess trying to do this. Besides, the mascara darkened the brown of her large almond-shaped eyes, managing to conceal the weary signs of last night's restless slumber.

She'd chosen to wear a pale yellow cotton blouse and matching shorts that brought out the chestnut highlights in her hair, brightening her slightly ruddy complexion. She thought enviously of Charlene's flawless porcelain skin, and sighed resignedly at her reflection.

She slid out of the truck, passing a quick final hand over her attire, and ventured toward the glass doors.

Charlene wasn't at her desk, and Lindsey stood for a few moments, muttering directives to her jumping stomach and pounding heart: *Will you please quiet down in there?!*

From beyond the side door she heard Max's low murmuring. It was followed by a girlish giggling. Lindsey waited for another few minutes, then when no one emerged, she turned toward the cushioned chairs behind her.

She sat down, wringing her prespiring hands together, crossing and uncrossing her legs. She picked up a magazine and flipped through it distractedly, the words and photographs making little impression on her.

"... and then Thea tells me Brian came home soaking wet, spouting: 'I caught the Admiral! I caught Wily Wilbur, Mom!'" Max chuckled. "And then he tells her he let the fish go. ''Cuz I knew he'd be homesick, just like Uncle Max!' he says."

Charlene laughed. "Uh-huh. Homesick, eh? Well, he's got a point, doesn't he?"

"Well, I for one believe my nephew. Wily Wilbur has been swimming Passamaquoddy Bay for—" His attention was suddenly diverted by Lindsey, who still sat clutching the magazine in her hand.

"Well! Look who's here. My first victim of the week." He strode over to her, smiling. He glanced at the magazine she was reading. "Ah, I see you're doing a little advance research for our fishing trip."

Lindsey looked down at the magazine in her hand, staring at the man in the photograph. He winked back at her as he demonstrated an overhand cast with his fishing rod. She folded the magazine quickly and slid it back onto the table.

"I doubt you'll catch anything in this city," said Charlene, frowning. "Not any Wily Wilburs, for certain."

"Maybe not. But I'm always up for new experiences," said Max, gesturing to Lindsey. "So, Lindsey McGinty, you ready for a new experience?"

Fishing? Or getting my tooth yanked? queried Lindsey silently. She obediently rose from her chair and nodded, exhaling a nervous breath. "I think so," she said with a strained smile.

Mrs. Honeysuckle was already in the room, a breeze of fastidiousness billowing from her brusque movements as she moved trays and rearranged equipment. She greeted Lindsey, her crisp white uniform making loud swishing noises as she directed their first patient to the chair.

"My, you look nice today, Miss McGinty," she said, draping a heavy leaden apron over Lindsey, pausing to pat her hand reassuringly. "Such a pretty outfit. Isn't she a pretty girl, Dr. Rupert?"

"Yes, she is," said Max, cocking his head, gazing at her for a prolonged moment before he left the room.

"Now, I'm just going to take some X rays of that tooth of yours. It's just to make sure there's no nerve damage."

Lindsey's stomach contracted queasily, but she managed a brave smile and a nod to show she understood. She hid her sweating palms beneath the lead apron.

"This'll only take a minute. Try not to move, now."

Lindsey froze, fixing her eyes on the Tolstoy "dental quote" above the doorway as the elderly woman arranged the equipment around her and left.

After what seemed an eternity of motionlessness, Max returned, grinning.

"The nerve is close," he told her, "but it doesn't look like it's going to be a problem."

Mrs. Honeysuckle entered carrying a tray laden with metal instruments. "So far so good." She winked at Lindsey.

Lindsey surveyed the contents of the tray, the color draining from her face as her eyes fell to the injection needle. "I, er—that needle—" She swallowed, feeling her limbs grow rigid, the muscles of her stomach suddenly bunching with apprehension.

Max and Mrs. Honeysuckle exchanged silent glances.

"Isn't there some way—any way—you could just knock me out?" said Lindsey, unable to keep the anxiety and fear out of her voice.

"Hmmm ... I could hit you over the head with a hammer, but I think you will agree that would be a tad more painful—if not a bit drastic." He quirked up an eyebrow. "It's just a little needle. You're not afraid of a little ol' needle, are you?"

The Electric Cupid 69

Lindsey's fingers curled into fists as she met his challenging gaze. "Okay, fine." *But make it quick,* she added mentally, tensing.

Max slipped his hand over her fist, gently prying loose her fingers. He squeezed her hand reassuringly. "Hey, trust me. I'm really good at this."

Lindsey stared into his eyes and at once found herself melting into that soft hazel-brown. Her body slowly began to relax against the leather of the chair.

Max snapped on his gloves, and leaned toward her. His subtle, musky scent wafted over her, seeping into her own pores like a sweet anesthetic. She closed her eyes as his face neared hers, and she felt his gloved fingers gently cup her chin as he rubbed on a topical with a Q-Tip.

"This'll numb up the skin for the injection," he explained.

The topical had a piña colada taste, immediately bringing to mind cool, calming blue waters. The light shining on her was the sun, warm and pleasant, bronzing her skin as she lay dozing on a white sandy beach....

The quick stinging prick of the needle stirred her calm blue waters into sudden violent, crashing waves, and Lindsey could feel her skin burning—

She snapped open her eyes.

"See? Not so bad, is it?" For an instant his mocking grin blocked out the light.

She glared up at him. But after a few seconds, she could feel numbness spreading into the left side of her cheek.

"Do your tongue and lip feel numb?" he asked her, his eyes crinkling at the corners.

"Yeth," said Lindsey. She glanced briefly over at the instruments on the tray, then shut her eyes tight. *Please let me get through this without screaming*, she pleaded silently. She forced her eyes open, hoping her expression appeared braver than how she was feeling.

"Now, what I'm going to do is rock the tooth back and

forth to loosen it,'' Max explained. ''You'll feel some pressure—like this.'' He pushed down hard on her shoulder, and Lindsey gazed up at him, a little startled.

But something in the way he looked at her, a tenderness that twinkled in his hazel-brown eyes, made her muscles uncoil, and her fingers unclench trustingly.

"Now, if you are feeling pain, I want you to raise your right hand."

Lindsey's right arm shot up.

Max frowned. "You feel pain?"

Lindsey grimaced apologetically. "Nervousss reactshon," she lisped, pulling her arm down and securing it with her other hand.

She watched him, noting the way his brow lowered and tightened into a straight line of concentration. The cleft in his chin held her for a moment, fascinating her. And her eyes meandered up to his lips, which pressed together, curving a little upward at the corners. At one point, their eyes met briefly, and Lindsey quickly flicked her gaze up at the ceiling, feeling vulnerable and trapped, but also strangely pleased by his close proximity.

The time flew by—or at least it did not feel to Lindsey as though she'd been lying there long when she heard the *pss-pop!* echo from inside her mouth, and Max's pleased: "Gotcha!"

Mrs. Honeysuckle smiled reassuringly at her and moved in to suction the gap where Lindsey's abscessed tooth had been.

"Okay," said Max cheerfully. "I'm going to put in some sutures to close up that hole." And immediately, upon seeing Lindsey's anxious look, he added. "Don't worry, it's just a couple of sutures. And no, you won't have to come back to get them out. They'll dissolve on their own in about ten days or so."

I won't have to come back? Relief flooded through her. But mingled with this relief, came something else. Was

The Electric Cupid 71

this—could this actually be *disappointment* she was feeling?

Mrs. Honeysuckle applied some gauze, and went into her post-op spiel, delivering a matronly, lecturelike speech:

"... no smoking, no rinsing, no using a straw for twenty-four hours, no spitting. Stay away from alcohol and spicy foods—and no hard candy for a couple of days," continued Mrs. Honeysuckle, her hands on her hips. "Unless, of course, you want to come back."

Lindsey glanced over at Max, who grinned at her impishly. *Had he read her thoughts just a moment ago?* She flushed and grinned back, a lopsided attempt at a grin, anyway.

"... warm-water rinse for healing purposes," the assistant went on. "You can take regular Tylenol for pain if you need to." She helped Lindsey to sit up.

"If you run out of gauze, we've found that using non-flavored tea bags will help." She reached in her mouth and changed the gauze. "Bite down now, Miss McGinty."

"You got all that?" said Max as Mrs. Honeysuckle gathered up her tray and with her practiced fastidiousness, began tidying up the room. Max pulled up his desk chair and sat down.

He consulted his watch. "I've got a few minutes before my next appointment, so if you don't mind, I'll keep you company for a few minutes while you get your, uh, bearings." He gazed at her, surveying her with an interested smile, his eyes openly curious.

And Lindsey realized she was leaning to her right, for the left side of her head felt oddly light, as if part of her weren't there.

"Sure," she managed, only it came out more like "shaar," as she balanced the gauze between her back molars.

"And no talking for at least thirty minutes, dear," said Mrs. Honeysuckle from the doorway.

Thirty minutes? Lindsey glanced at her watch; she had to be at Greycan Industries in twenty minutes. If it weren't an emergency job she might've followed Harry's advice and taken the day off. But Tim was on holidays, and Mike and the others were still working out in Beacon Hill.

"She's great, isn't she?" said Max as Mrs. Honeysuckle departed in a starched *crackle-swish* of movement down the hall to the back offices. "You can just nod—lift up your left hand if I'm beginning to bore you, or if you want me to shut up."

Lindsey shook her head, frowned, then nodded, gazing down at her clasped hands. *I like your company,* she wanted to say.

They chatted—or rather, Max talked and Lindsey nodded intermittently, occasionally stretching her lips into a numbed, clumsy smile.

She liked the sound of his voice, rich and even in its vernacular tone—different from her own clipped Bostonian accent. And when he spoke of Saint Andrews, she did not fail to notice the bright nostalgic sparkle that lit his hazel-brown eyes. Lindsey listened attentively, storing away tidbits about his family: parents who owned and ran a local New Brunswick grocery store, three sisters—all married, with two nieces and a nephew between them.

"Actually, Thea's coming down to Boston for a visit in a couple of weeks. She's bringing her son, Brian. Great kid." He smiled. "You like children?"

Lindsey nodded; Brian was the one who claimed to have caught Wily Wilbur, she recalled.

"That Brian is growing up to be some fisherman." He laughed. "Speaking of fishing—how about this Saturday?"

Lindsey's eyebrows shot up inquiringly.

"You're free this Saturday?"

She gazed at him, not understanding, but she found herself nodding all the same.

"Good. I've got an extra fishing pole you can use," he

said, leaning forward in his chair. He rubbed the cleft in his chin. "I'll pick you up at five-thirty."

In the morning? Her eyes widened with her silent question.

Max chuckled at her reaction. "The early fisherman catches the best fish," he intoned. "That way, we can laze about in the boat for the rest of the day. Get to know each other," he added with a grin. "I notice Boston seems to get awfully hot around midday, so you'd better bring along a hat. And I'll pack us a lunch—"

"How's it going in here?" Charlene swept into the room. She glanced sharply in Lindsey's direction, then turned to Max, standing between them, as if to intentionally sever the thread of their conversation. "Thea's on the phone, Max. I transferred the call to your office. And your next patient's on his way."

Lindsey slid off the chair as Max rose, nodding.

Charlene turned then and smiled at Lindsey. "I'll walk you out, Miss McGinty." And the receptionist's hand was already on her arm, the tips of her pink-painted nails pinching Lindsey's skin.

"See you Wednesday!" Max called after her.

Wednesday? *Oh,* Lindsey remembered. *The high-hat lights.*

Charlene brusquely ushered Lindsey through to the waiting room. "That tooth is bringing you a lot of business," she commented. "It's nice that Max is meeting new business contacts."

A business contact. Was that what she was to Max? wondered Lindsey. For some reason this thought left her with a strange feeling of disappointment.

"Now, take care of that tooth. We don't want to see you back here any time soon," said Charlene, sounding suddenly cheerful. "If *we're* still here, that is," she added, moving behind the desk.

What did she mean, "if we're still here"? Lindsey

mulled these words over in her mind as she unlocked the Toyota and slid into the driver's seat. Was Max actually considering returning to Saint Andrews?

Had she missed something? For she'd received no such impression from Max. On the contrary; he seemed quite intent on staying here in Boston, slowly establishing a clientele of patients, making renovations to his house, although . . .

Lindsey could not dismiss the nostaglic look that misted his expression whenever he spoke about his Canadian home. And his sister and nephew were coming to visit him. Perhaps nostalgia and homesickness might push him to move back to the place of his fondest memories, where his family was, and where he could fish—

Fishing. They were going fishing this Saturday, Lindsey suddenly remembered.

A new hope gripped her. If he saw that Boston wasn't just a bustling city, that amid all the skyscrapers and busy factories, there were indeed places where one could fish: Turtle Pond, the McCorckle Fishing Pier, City Point—

What was she doing? Figuring out ways to convince Max to stay here in Boston? If he wanted to leave, he would, and she couldn't stop him. Certainly not by being a travel guide, and definitely not by trying to transform Boston into Saint Andrews. It was his childhood home, after all, and there he had real ties—family that loved him; here, he was a stranger, literally a fish out of water.

And what did she care anyway? She barely knew this man. The same gust of wind that had brought him into her life could just as easily sweep him away again. Like a quick handshake: "Hi, how are you? Nice meeting you. So long." No tearful good-byes. No harm done. No exchange of electricity.

But there had been electricity—at least, she'd felt some kind of spark. But had he felt it too?

As Lindsey turned down Arlington Street, her limbs tingled and her chest felt heavy with anxiety—no, not anxiety, but longing, a yearning that filled her, suddenly making her break out into a slow sweat.

Her thoughts suddenly drifted back to a lecture she'd attended at MIT. It was one of the few lectures that had stuck in her mind, surfacing from time to time to come back to haunt her—to taunt her.

The professor had spoken about human life and electricity, and how the two were inextricably bound together. Even as she'd sat there listening to him, he'd explained how tiny electric signals were spreading through her heart muscle, triggering and coordinating her individual heartbeats.

And it was these signals that could be detected by metal sensors, a kind of "echo" sent through the body tissue to the skin. " 'Echoes of the Heart,' " is what I call them," the professor had joked.

Lindsey's hand went to her chest. And even as she did this she could feel her body humming beneath her palm like a machine engine. Her heart beat swift and strong, echoing messages throughout her body. It was a Morse code telling her that regardless of whether Max left Boston, or decided to stay—she was, indeed, mysteriously but undeniably, attracted to this man.

"Three weeks in paradise! This time tomorrow we'll be lazing on a white sandy beach, gazing out at the Atlantic Ocean," Rhonda twirled around happily. "Imagine, sipping piña coladas, Hawaiian Punch—"

"It's the *Pacific* Ocean, Rhonda," Lindsey pointed out. "And twenty-four hours from now it'll be four-thirty in the morning in paradise."

"You're such a stickler for details." Rhonda glanced around the room frantically. "Where's my tote bag? Honey!" she called downstairs. "Is my tote bag down there?"

A muffled assent drifted up.

Rhonda rummaged through her purse. "Wallet, Pepto-Bismol, sunscreen—my sunglasses. Where're my sunglasses?"

"On your head," said Lindsey, smiling.

"Oh." Rhonda's hand patted them, and she exhaled loudly. "I guess we're all set." She swept a final gaze about the bedroom.

"What am I going to do without you for three weeks?" said Lindsey.

Rhonda reached over and hugged her friend tightly. "You're going to go fishing with that handsome dentist of yours." She squeezed Lindsey's hands, and gazed sternly at her friend's uncertain expression. "Be adventurous for once in your life, Lindsey. Follow your heart. And who knows? It might just lead you to *your* paradise."

"I'm fine right where I am, thank you," muttered Lindsey.

"Uh-huh." Rhonda nodded, pressing her lips together. "You're afraid to let yourself fall in love." And she smiled demurely. "Trust me, Lindsey. Romance is wonderful."

"Rhonda! Come on!" Rick shouted from downstairs. "We're going to be late for our flight!"

Rhonda rolled her eyes in exasperation. "He's been saying that all morning. As soon as we get there, I'm hiding his watch and alarm clock. I mean, who takes an alarm clock on a vacation?"

She drew a breath and fingered her earrings. "Hey, you haven't said anything about my new earrings."

Lindsey gazed at the large happy-faced suns that dangled from the long silver chains. "They're perfect." She grinned. She glanced down at her plain T-shirt and shorts, her hand touching her earringless ears. She sighed. "Why can't I be stylish like you, Rhonda?"

"You?" Rhonda smiled. "Lindsey, you have your own style."

Rick's voice boomed from downstairs. "Rho-onda-a!"

Rhonda chewed on her lip. "Okay, you have all the instructions, right? You just have to water the plants on Wednesday and Saturday. There's tons of food in the fridge, and plenty to drink. If you want to invite Max over—"

"Rhonda," Lindsey interrupted her, holding up her hands.

"Well, whatever. You've got the house key?"

Lindsey steered her out of the bedroom and into the hall. "Yes. Everything's under control, Rhonda. Don't worry."

Rhonda laughed as they hurriedly descended the stairs and strode to the front entrance. "Oh, I'm not worried." She jerked her thumb at the house next door. "After all, we've got the Watchful Widow, Madame Nosy, to look out for us."

Lindsey tracked the path of Rhonda's thumb and spied the pale oval face peering at them from the side window. It abruptly disappeared behind a hasty rustle of the curtains. Lindsey grinned. "I guess I'd better watch myself," she said.

Rhonda put her arm around her friend. "Promise me one thing?"

"Anything," said Lindsey.

"You won't chicken out on this fishing trip."

"I—I won't," Lindsey promised. But her heart gave a tiny questioning beat behind her rib cage. She didn't tell Rhonda she'd been having second thoughts about the trip.

Rick was glancing at his watch nervously. "Let's go, honeybun. That plane's not going to wait forever, you know."

"It doesn't leave for another hour and a half," grumbled Rhonda. She turned to Lindsey. "Thanks for looking after the house, Lindsey. We'll be thinking about you in Hawaii."

"Well, don't think too hard. You're supposed to be on vacation," she reminded them. "Go on! I'll lock up here."

She waved after them from the doorstep, watching them until they turned down the street. After a quick survey of the upstairs and the kitchen, she locked the door behind her.

The phone rang as she started down the steps. Lindsey paused, then ran back up, quickly unlocked the door and skidded into the kitchen, picking up the phone in mid-ring.

"Hello?" she said breathlessly.

"Hello, may I speak to Lindsey McGinty?"

Lindsey's heart lurched as she recognized the voice.

"This-this is she," she said, struggling to compose herself.

"Oh, hi. This is Max."

Yes, I know, she replied silently.

"Uh, Max—Max Rupert?"

"Yes, er, hi. How did—?"

"Your friend Rhonda gave me this number," he explained. "She said you were looking after their place."

"Yes." Naturally, Rhonda had conveniently forgotten to tell her she'd spoken to Max. She waited.

"So how's the tooth?"

Lindsey touched her cheek. A phantom pain, like a memory suddenly stirring, coursed through her jaw. "I'm still alive."

Max chuckled. "I haven't had a patient die on me yet. I hope it's changed your mind about dentists. We're not really all that dangerous."

I wouldn't say that, Lindsey retorted to herself.

"Anyway, why I'm calling—uh, about tomorrow. I was wondering if you could come by the house a little later . . . say twoish?"

"Sure." Harry hadn't booked her for anything else that afternoon.

"Great."

There was a long pause.

Lindsey cleared her throat. "I'll see you tomorrow, around two, then," she said.

"Looking forward to it. Well . . . bye, Lindsey."

Lindsey hung up the phone, her thoughts buzzing, and for a moment she forgot where she was. With heart thumping, she quickly recovered herself and strode out of the kitchen, making her way back down the hall to the front door. She hesitated before the large gilt mirror.

Her reflection stared back at her, surprise splaying into derision as she saw the two telltale spots of color on her cheeks. Lindsey frowned at herself, but it did not suppress the bright glow in her dark brown eyes. Impulsively she ran her fingers through her short pixie-cut hair, flung open the door, and locked it behind her.

Chapter Six

Lindsey stared at the note tacked on the door:

Lindsey,
  Let yourself in. Will be back around three. Key's under the mat.

Max

Lindsey glanced around, as if expecting to see a lineup of burglars leaping out from behind her. She took down the note and checked under the welcome mat. The key was there. She shook her head and unlocked the door. Maybe the folk in Saint Andrews were more trusting, but here in Boston—

As she tentatively stepped inside, she nearly tripped over a metal rectangular box. She gripped her own toolbox, and immediately spied the two fishing poles leaning against the far wall. Lindsey stared at them.

One was paint-flecked, bent slightly in the same manner a much-used hockey stick might be curved to suit its owner. The other rod glistened, its robins's egg-blue color shiny and untouched. It looked suspiciously new.

Had Max gone out and bought this fishing pole—just for her?

Lindsey immediately dismissed this thought and strode into the kitchen. But her gaze lingered for a moment, roving toward the living room and dining area.

A new love seat and couch occupied the corner of the

living room, a muted jade and blue color that showed off a darker green ottoman. There were no other pieces of furniture, except an antique-looking bookcase which had yet to be filled with books. Lindsey was quick to notice the crowd of photographs; a blown-up portrait of one in particular caught her immediate attention.

The woman in the photograph stared back at her, striking a sophisticated, contemplative pose, reminding Lindsey of one of those glamorous 1940s movie stars.

How many photographs of Charlene did Max have? she wondered. One might almost think that the receptionist lived here.

Lindsey forced her attention back to her toolbox and advanced toward the kitchen. But as she set her equipment down and glanced at her watch, curiosity gripped her. She paused, chewing on her lip.

"Don't be a snoop," she scolded herself aloud; for in her head was a nagging thought, nudging, dragging her toward a place where she knew she shouldn't go.

"Just a peek. A quick peek," she said, even as she tiptoed around the corner and skulked down the long, high-ceilinged corridor.

She glanced into the two rooms on the left, traipsed past the bathroom, and paused at the room on her right. They were empty. But the last door to her right was closed. Lindsey heard the loud creak of the hardwood beneath her feet, and cringed, glancing furtively behind her.

"Just a quick peek," she repeated under her breath. Her heart throbbed in her throat, her fingers damp as they turned the doorknob.

His familiar, pleasant after-shave swept over her, and she hesitated, blinking, filling her nostrils with the alluring scent.

Her gaze moved immediately to the bed. She took in the pillows stacked up on the side closest to her, the indented imprint of his head still there. A forest-green duvet was thrust back carelessly to reveal matching sheets. Lindsey's hand reached out to touch the sheet, almost expecting it to still be warm with his presence. She immediately shrank back, chastising herself.

What are you doing?

Her eyes surveyed then the paperbacks stacked on the bedside table. She swept a cursory glance at the titles of the books on the bedside table: *Catch-22, Madame Bovary, The Dubliners*, a dog-geared edition of *Anna Karenina*. Lindsey remembered the quote above the doorway in his office, and gave a low chuckle.

She spied then the opened book, lying facedown between the folds of the duvet. She leaned over the bed, wanting to see its title, wondering what kind of material would interest this man. Mystery? Adventure? A thriller, maybe. She turned her head so she could read the title. She muffled a gasp of surprise.

"Electricity and Magnetism: The Invisible Energy," she read aloud. Lindsey had the same copy in her own bookshelves. It was an in-depth manifesto, dry, but informative—and required reading for MIT students.

Her foot prodded something sticking out from under the bed. She glanced down, and bent to inspect it when she heard the sound of a key in the front door.

Lindsey bolted upright, her chest constricting, her breath frozen in her throat. She swiftly retreated, shut the door, and loped back down the corridor. However, before she could return safely to the kitchen, Charlene swung the door open.

They stared at each other, Lindsey's face mirroring Charlene's look of surprise and astonishment.

But it was Charlene who recovered herself first. Her smile was slow, not reaching the green catlike eyes.

"I'm sorry if I startled you. I didn't know Max was home already," she said, closing the door. "Although I didn't see his car—" Her eyes suddenly fastened on the fishing poles.

"He's not home. I, er, let myself in."

Charlene tore her gaze from the rods and frowned. "He left the door unlocked?"

"No, he left the key under the mat."

The crease between Charlene's brows deepened. For an instant she looked at Lindsey as if she didn't believe her. "Well, you better give me the key," she said coldly.

"It's on the table," said Lindsey. The chilliness of her own tone surprised her, and she could feel her competitive instincts suddenly springing into action. What was it about this woman that made her react so?

Charlene moved past her into the kitchen, saw the key, and picked it up. "Max can be a little too trusting at times," she said, not as an apology, but more as a statement of fact.

Lindsey said nothing. She moved to her toolbox and flipped open the latches.

"You just arrived, then?" asked Charlene, watching her.

"Just a couple of minutes before you did." She gazed at her tools and noted with chagrin she'd left her stud finder and template in her other toolbox.

"Forget something?" Charlene eyed her. "I don't see why he thinks he needs more light in this room," she said, gazing up at the ceiling. "Or was this your idea?"

"No. He asked me to put in these high-hat lights."

Charlene shook her head. "Wasted money." She went to the refrigerator, extracted a bottle of juice, but did not offer one to Lindsey.

"Be back in a minute," murmured Lindsey, striding quickly out of the kitchen. She heard Charlene pick up the phone and begin to dial.

As she rummaged around the back of her cab, trying to find her stud finder, Max's Chevrolet ambled up the driveway. He waved to her. Lindsey waved back and promptly dropped her template on the road. With her face heating up, she bent to retrieve it as Max parked in front of the house. She heard the car door open and slam shut just as she spotted the stud finder. When Lindsey turned, she saw Max standing there, waiting for her midway up the front path.

"Hi," he greeted her with a grin. "You found the key all right?"

Lindsey nodded.

"Sorry I wasn't here. Had to go buy a couple of beds for my guests."

Guests? Lindsey gazed at him.

He noticed then Charlene's Taurus parked on the side of the street. "Hmmm . . . another guest." He let out a sigh. "My sister and her son are coming to visit next week." Max ran his hand through his hair. "I have this feeling they're going to try to convince me to come back to Saint Andrews."

And how much convincing will you need? Lindsey asked silently, sneaking a sideways look at him. *He looks tired*, she thought. *And distracted.*

"Thea, my sister—she still thinks of me as her little brother. Last time I spoke to her, she lectured me for a half hour about proper eating habits. She has this preconceived notion that all bachelors are too lazy to cook for themselves—that all we do is defrost TV dinners." He laughed.

Lindsey gave a low chuckle. "Sounds like my parents. They send me a 'vitamin' package every few months from Florida. And every few months or so, I get these huge crates of oranges. They seem to have forgotten that we get fruit up here, too, in Boston."

"Well, you can't blame them for worrying. A woman on her own in a big city—"

"Would they worry less if I were a man?" she retorted, her eyes flashing at him. "Believe it or not, we single women are more than capable of taking care of ourselves."

Max grinned. "Oh, I don't doubt that for a second," he said, opening the door for her. "But I bet your parents are hoping that one day you'll meet that special someone and settle down—"

"Well! There you are! Max, where've you been?" Charlene greeted him at the door, her hands on her hips. "You didn't go out shopping for those beds without me, did you?"

Max shrugged. "The beds'll be here tomorrow."

"But, Max, I thought—" Charlene furrowed her brow in irritation. Her narrowed catlike eyes flickered in Lindsey's direction, signaling to Lindsey that she was intruding on this domestic dispute.

But Max ignored Charlene's annoyed display and bent down to retrieve the rectangular box, a smile lighting his face. "Ah, I better get my tackle box out of the way, here. I was just making sure I had enough leader and floats for Saturday."

"I heard it might rain on Saturday," said Charlene.

"Ah, we can handle a little rain, eh, Lindsey?"

Lindsey smiled uncertainly and moved awkwardly past Charlene, conscious of the loud tromping footfalls her boots made on the floor. She glanced down at Charlene's tiny delicate feet, toenails painted a perfect pink, the heeled sandals accentuating her slim, shapely ankles.

As Lindsey measured and began saw-drilling the holes in the ceiling, she overheard Charlene and Max arguing in one of the rooms down the hall.

"... wish you'd consulted me first."

"Charlene, I'm capable of making my own decisions...." Lindsey could hear Charlene moving about the room. "Yes," said Max, "that's a good idea. You can arrange it, if you like ... Thea won't mind ..."

"... you call your parents? You know, Thea told me they still don't have a dentist to fill your place, Max."

"There's plenty of good dentists in that area, Charlene. What about Bernie Grospin?"

". . . all miss you. Brian's been asking about you constantly—and little Nettie and Grace . . ."

Lindsey let the conversation drift past her ears, and tried to dispel the tension that enveloped her, invading her concentration.

Twice she very nearly spliced the lead wires and almost dropped the high-hat light. If only Charlene would leave, she thought; for it seemed to Lindsey that with every new encounter, that woman turned the tension knob up just a little more. Indeed, the tension level in the house was strung so tautly, Lindsey was afraid to make any sudden moves lest she break something. And even as she thought this, Lindsey could feel those green eyes boring holes through the wall and watching her with that unveiled suspicion. *Why,* wondered Lindsey, *would she be suspicious of me? But wait—*

Could Charlene actually be . . . *jealous*—of *her*? But why? Charlene was so delicate and beautiful, poised, confident. And Lindsey'd seen the way Lenny had looked at Charlene that night she and Max had rescued them—the way the other electricians at the fair hadn't been able to tear their eyes away from her doll-like beauty. Surely, Charlene could see Lindsey was no threat to her?

And yet, too, Lindsey had not failed to notice Max's flippant, almost cavalier attitude toward Charlene. To Lindsey, his actions were more consistent with that of an affectionate brother than a romantic partner.

But could this merely be wishful thinking on my part? wondered Lindsey. For she and Max had known each other for less than two weeks. They were, in fact, virtual strangers. How could he possibly have developed any feelings for her in that short a time?

Lindsey chewed on her lip and frowned, willing these thoughts away.

However, as she returned to her task—determined to complete the job before evening fell—one single thought still teetered on the edge of her mind:

How could she—a successful single woman, a woman who was not given to surrendering her heart without a fight—have any feelings for *him?*

Lindsey stirred the spaghetti sauce, lifted the wooden spoon to her lips, and tasted her concoction. The rhythmic *rat-tat-tat-! tat-tat!* on her door startled her out of her thoughts. Her hand jerked, and the sauce splooshed onto her T-shirt.

"Darn!" she muttered. "Door's open! Come on i—"

"Hey-ho! Lindsey girl!" Lenny let himself in. He sniffed the air. "Hmmm . . . somethin' smells good."

"Hi, Lenny." She rubbed at the tomato stain on her T-shirt. "What's up?"

Lenny hitched up his jeans and smoothed down his wiry cowlick. He glanced around the apartment nervously, almost shyly. "I, uh, came to ask you for some advice."

"Oh?" Lindsey looked up. She'd assumed he'd smelled her cooking and was looking for an invitation to dinner.

"Spaghetti, huh? Gee, Lindsey, I didn't know you could cook."

"I'm a woman of many talents." She glanced at the jar of ready-made "home-cooked" pasta sauce, and smiled to herself.

Lenny rubbed his stomach and slumped down on her couch. "Haven't eaten a thing since this morning," he said.

"Okay." Lindsey sighed, grinning. "How do you like your spaghetti?"

"I don't know if I could eat just right now." Lenny leaned forward and cupped his face in his hands.

Lindsey furrowed her brow curiously. What was this she was detecting in her neighbor's voice? Misery? Despair? "Lenny? You okay?"

"Yes—no. No, I'm not okay." He rubbed his face, staring down at the steel toes of his cowboy boots. "I need your advice." He looked up at her. "I mean, you're a woman," he added, as if this explained everything.

Lindsey cocked a brow and sat down next to him. "Yes, it's true. I am a woman."

"This is serious."

She took in his irritated look. "Okay, sorry. Shoot."

Lenny kneaded his fingers together, his gaze returning to rest again on the toes of his boots. "You see, there's this woman at the office. She just started there this week—Miranda Caulfield. I-I can't get her out of my mind."

Lindsey tried to mask her surprise. But in all these years she'd known Lenny, she'd never once imagined Lenny ever really falling in love. Oh, he'd dogged her for months, trying to get her to go out with him, but Lindsey could see by the way his shoulders slumped forward dejectedly, the dispirited, confused gleam in his eyes, that this was different than his puppy-doglike infatuation for her.

Love could do crazy things to a person—even to Lenny, she realized.

She listened to his voice grow more impassioned as he went on, describing this woman through love-glazed eyes. Evidently, Miranda Caulfied was a cross between Raquel Welch and Marilyn Monroe: a woman who had "the face an angel" and "the body of a goddess."

"She's interesting, too. She likes going to football games, and even *understands* it. She can pick off baseball stats—batting averages, pitching stats—right off the top of her head. Just like that." He snapped his fingers, his face glowing. "And she can shuffle a deck of cards like a real pro."

Yeah, that's Marilyn Monroe all right, thought Lindsey.

"So why don't you just ask this girl out, Lenny?"

Lenny grimaced. "I-I can't. I get all ... funny inside

The Electric Cupid

everytime I even *think* about asking her out." He pressed his hands to his belly.

"Well, you talk to her, don't you?"

"Yeah. About baseball and football. We even played poker twice on our break."

"Then, why don't you ask her to a baseball game or something?"

"What if she says no?"

"Is she seeing anyone? She's not married, is she?"

Lenny shook his head. "I asked Patti. She's not seeing anyone. But I don't know if she likes me." He gazed imploringly at Lindsey. "I was wondering if you could—"

"Ask her if she likes you? What is this? Lenny, you're not in high school anymore. You're a good-looking . . . er, confident guy. You have . . . a lot to offer a woman. A girl would be crazy to turn you down."

"You did. Several times as I recall."

Lindsey sighed. "Lenny, we're friends."

"That's what I told that guy—Max? You know, your, uh, dentist?"

Lindsey straightened, her stomach muscles tightening all of a sudden. "Oh?" she said quietly. *Max was asking about me?*

"Yeah. We played questions and answers after you left that night. That guy sure seemed interested in you." He took in her stricken expression and quickly added: "Hey, I didn't tell him anything too embarassing. He thought you and I—well, I told him we lived in the same house, but that there was nothing between us—that we were only friends."

"And what'd he say?" The question tumbled out before she could stop herself.

Lenny grinned slyly at her. "You like this guy, huh?"

Lindsey flushed. "He's—he's all right."

"Was that his sister with him, then? She was quite the dish—oh, excuse me. I didn't mean—"

Lindsey waved a dismissive hand. "That's okay. Charlene is quite beautiful."

"Yeah, but..." Lenny inclined his head, gazing at Lindsey. "She's not you. You've got something—I don't know, something special. You're... different."

Different? "Thanks." Lindsey smiled. "I think."

Lenny rubbed his chin. "So you think I might have a shot with Miranda?"

"I say, go for it! Take the risk, Lenny. You don't know until you ask her out, right? And if she says no, then, well, at least you'll know she wasn't the right woman for you." Lindsey squeezed his burly shoulder and stood up. "And then you can quit torturing yourself."

"So, what about you?"

"What about me?"

"You and this Max guy. It's pretty obvious he's got a thing for you." He grinned. "And seeing that look on your face a moment ago, I gather the feeling is mutual."

"I don't know—"

"Hey—ho! What were you just telling me about going for it—'take the risk'? Aren't those the words you used?"

"But it's different—"

"Because you're a woman? Man, I'd love it if a woman asked *me* out."

"Actually"—Lindsey bit her lip—"we're going fishing this weekend—tomorrow, in fact."

Now, as she thought about this, it seemed almost more like a week, not two days, since she'd last spoken to Max. And she'd left rather abruptly from his house that day, Charlene's hawklike presence practically pushing her out the door before she could confirm their fishing date.

"But it's not like it's an official date or anything," she added quickly.

"It's that other woman, isn't it?"

Lindsey regarded him, surprised. "I don't know what—"

Lenny laughed. "If I were him, I'd tell you to stop worrying. He's got his eye on *you*, not her."

I wouldn't be too sure about that, said Lindsey silently, strolling into the kitchen. But Lenny's words had given her step a sudden new buoyancy. She reached above her in the cupboard and pulled down a pot.

"Spaghetti?"

Lenny rose from the couch and rubbed his belly, a wide grin breaking across his face. "Yeah, I'm starved."

Chapter Seven

The dawn light splayed pinkish yellow across her rumpled sheets. Lindsey yawned, slid out of bed, and zipped up her jeans. She blinked at the lingering twilight that shadowed the corners of her bedroom. Her clock ticked loudly next to her bed: 5:20 A.M.

"Okay, I'm up," she told it aloud. She still had ten minutes to shake off this morning daze, to make herself presentable. Coffee—she needed coffee.

Plodding into the kitchen, she turned on her coffee machine. It gave an involuntary shudder, sputtered, then settled into silence.

"Oh, no. Don't break down on me now." She thumped it and rubbed her eyes, groaning a sigh. She drew back the curtains and glanced out the window, keeping an eye out for Max's Chevrolet.

Not here yet. *Good,* she thought, running her fingers through her short hair. She closed her eyes and stood there for a moment, enjoying the silence of the house.

A car engine roused her, and her heart revved into motion with the sound. She watched the brown Chevrolet sidle up behind her truck. The outline of the figure behind the wheel glowed palely in the early dawn light. Lindsey saw him pause for a moment, then lean toward the passenger seat, and pass his hand over his hair, quickly brushing his fingers over his face in last-minute inspection before he climbed out.

Lindsey leaped out of her dreamy state and sprang into

action. Blood rushed to her head, leaving her fingers and toes to tingle with nervous excitement. She grabbed her knapsack, pausing for a moment to catch her breath.

"You're only going fishing, Lindsey," she told herself, pressing her hand to her chest, trying to quieten the clamoring inside.

She reached down and pulled back the lid of the cooler. Ice. She'd forgotten the ice. She ran back into the kitchen and pulled out the ice bags. As she packed them alongside the cans of root beer (darn! she'd forgotten to buy juice), she heard the gentle rapping at the door.

Lindsey froze and stared at the door.

Another knock, more loudly this time.

Lindsey unlocked the chain latch and opened the door.

"Good morning," greeted Max with a smile. "I was afraid you might still be sleeping."

"No. I-I'm awake." Lindsey stifled a yawn and adjusted her knapsack about her shoulders. She bent down to secure the lid of the cooler.

"Hey, you didn't have to bring anything. I told you I had everything covered."

"It's just some drinks. I was going to make sandwiches—" *But I forgot to buy bread,* she added, avoiding his gaze. *How can someone be so chipper and look so great this early in the morning?* she thought, slightly irritated.

She smoothed out the sleeves of her bulky sweatshirt and ran her hands down the hips of her worn jeans, wishing now she'd gotten up early enough to jump in the shower—and maybe selected a more attractive outfit.

With a quick surreptitious glance, she took in his loose bibbed pants and the white T-shirt that showed off the lean curve of his bicep. He looked as though he'd just stepped out of one of those fishing magazines, only a tad more clean cut, and a little less predatory—except for the way he was staring at her now—

"Here, let me take that." He gestured to the cooler.

But Lindsey was already hefting the cooler, and she barred his way, forcing him to retreat. She heard him exhale a sigh, and he shook his head in a half shrug, starting down the front walkway.

Lindsey locked the door, a process that took a few minutes because of the rusted jamb she'd yet to have taken time to replace. Why was it that she had plenty of time to fix other people's things, and not her own?

Max opened the backseat and let her shove the cooler inside. But as she strode over to the passenger side, he was already there, holding open the door for her. He grinned at her as she slid inside; it was a smug grin that said: "I'm going to be chivalrous whether you like it or not."

They drove through the hushed neighborhood, accompanied only by the first songs of the rising thrush and the early rustlings of eager squirrels already on the hunt. Lindsey relaxed against the seat, and closed her eyes, drinking in the complex, musky scent that mingled intoxicatingly with the cool morning air. She yawned, her sigh of contentment rising in the silence, drifting . . .

"Coffee?"

Lindsey snapped open her eyes and jerked herself upright as if all of a sudden aware of his presence. She looked at the coffee thermos as if it were an alien thing.

"Oh. You don't drink coffee either?

Either? "No, er, actually, I'd love some," said Lindsey, taking it from him clumsily. "You don't drink coffee?"

"Me?" He laughed. "I wouldn't be able to function without it. But Charlene, she's got this thing about caffeine. Everything she drinks is caffeine-free."

The mention of Charlene's name had an immediate sobering affect on Lindsey's mood, and she could feel her teeth grinding as she unscrewed the top. All of a sudden Charlene's territorial presence was stalking through the car, settling between them like a cautionary guardrail. A knot began to form in the pit of her stomach, causing the muscles in her shoulders to tense a little.

Even with the woman's absence, she managed to stress out Lindsey.

Max cleared his throat. "I rented a boat—"

"A boat?" Charlene's guardrail lifted and slowly began to evaporate.

Max glanced at her, eyebrows raised. "Yes. You're not afraid of getting into a boat with me, are you?"

No, not with you, she answered silently. "I just thought—" All those pictures in the magazines she'd bought had men casting their fishing lines safely from banks of rivers.

"You have something against boats?" he inquired, smiling.

"No, of course not," she replied quickly. *It's just that I've never been out on a boat before,* she added, grimacing inwardly.

"You'll love it. Hmmm . . . drifting along the river . . . just you and the sound of the water." His smile grew wistful. "I don't think I could live not being near the water. There's something so . . . calming, so soothing about it. And yet, there's still that element of wildness, that unpredictability—" He glanced over at her, a vague look of embarassment crossing his face.

"Sorry. Didn't mean to break out into rhapsody there. I've been a little—overly nostalgic lately."

"No, it's okay. I think I understand," said Lindsey. *You miss Saint Andrews.*

She gazed at him, unself-consciously now, admiring the way the sun's early-morning rays radiated off his smooth high forehead and illuminated his strong nose, warming the upturned lips. And for an instant, as his expression turned pensive, she glimpsed the shimmer of gold in his eyes.

You're interesting, she found herself thinking. *And maybe a little too good-looking,* she added, touching the cool back of her hand to her hot cheek. She sipped the coffee from the plastic cup and forced her attention away from him.

From the passenger window she spied the sleepy occupants slumped behind the wheels of passing cars, operating on automatic pilot, oblivious to her watchful gaze. And suddenly, Lindsey felt wide awake, energy seeming to zip through her like an electrical current.

Whether it was the coffee, or just the morning air, she could not rightly tell. But she suspected this sudden energy had more to do with this man next her. Indeed, his proximity seemed to generate some kind of kinetic field, sparking in her a nervous excitement that jangled her nerves and made her all the more aware of her own body.

She realized as they finally arrived at the Stony Brook parkgrounds, that neither of them had spoken, and that she had found herself enjoying, even relaxing in the comfort of his thoughtful presence.

And perhaps in sensing this as well, Max suddenly turned to her, his eyes flickering searchingly over her face: "It's nice to be with someone and not feel like you have to, you know . . . talk."

Oh! Lindsey immediately wondered, *Does he think me dull?* A nervous anxiety swelled in her chest. "I like to talk," she intoned quickly, forcing a cheerful, sunny look on her face. "Sometimes you can't get me to shut up." But even as she blurted this out, she could feel her insides groaning. *Why'd you have to go and spoil the moment?*

Max blinked at her, his straight brows knitting together in momentary confusion. But then the corner of his mouth curved upward slightly, and he shook his head, turning his gaze to the man approaching them from the kiosk.

"Always the competitor, huh?" he muttered low under his breath.

Lindsey bit her lip. Why did she always manage to say the wrong thing at the wrong time? And he was right about

The Electric Cupid

her being competitive. Growing up with two athletic brothers, who were not only varsity superstars, but honor roll students, had brought her up with this natural instinct to compete; it was a reaction Lindsey had culled from years of trying to keep up with her brothers, while at the same time maintaining her independence.

"Lindsey, not everything has to be a competition, you know," Rhonda had once pointed out to her. "You always seem to be trying to prove something. Why don't you just relax and be yourself?"

Be myself? As simple as it sounded, Lindsey found her friend's advice difficult to follow, for as Lindsey soon realized, this instinct to compete could not easily be quashed—especially when she was around men. And even more noticeably, around men she was attracted to.

Max was speaking to the park ranger, and the man in the brown uniform pointed past the kiosk, indicating where the boat rental was. He tipped his hat at Lindsey.

"Morning, ma'am." He smiled a white toothy smile. "Enjoy your day."

Max nosed the Chevrolet past the kiosk, turning down the graveled road. "I don't think he sees many women coming up here to fish."

"Fishing is a man's sport, is it?" Her tone was more harsh than she intended.

"Maybe in these parts, but not in Saint Andrews," said Max, shrugging. "I know plenty of women who like to fish—and who are good at it, too," he added.

Like Charlene? wondered Lindsey, and all at once she could feel that old competitive streak resurfacing within her. *If Charlene can fish, I can fish. Just watch me,* she thought with a determined grimace.

She watched closely as Max demonstrated how to slip the crimp over the end of the leader. Her eyes noted the easy deftness of his fingers as he looped the line through the eye of the swivel and back into the metal sleeve of the crimp. He squeezed the crimp with metal pliers, and finally attached the hook.

"Think you can do it?"

Lindsey pursed her lips and nodded. "I figured out how to use the reel, didn't I?"

"Hmmm . . . the rod and reel, yes, are important," he said, "but it's the performance of your tackle—the leaders, crimps, beads, and swivels—they're really what count in the end. The way you present them, use them." He grinned. "If you like, think of them as a kind of . . . mating dance."

"Mating dance?"

Max regarded her, chuckling under his breath. He leaned nearer, observing her for a brief moment. "It's the natural law of things. It's just a matter of luring your prey by showing off your best equipment."

He handed her the red-and-white floater. "Women do it all the time," he added with a teasing glint in his eye. "They wear perfume, makeup, high heels—" His gaze took in her bulky sweatshirt, her jeans, and sneakers. "Or even better, they try to hide their assets—which makes men even crazier."

"Men can make women crazy as well," murmured Lindsey, her nostrils flaring slightly as his spicy, musky scent wafted around her, circling her like a tantalizing mist. She could hear the slow steady rhythm of his breathing and found herself trying to match it. But her heart was pumping a little too fast, and she quickly abandoned this, dizzily gulping for air.

As he handed her the crimp, his fingers brushed hers, and they both suddenly recoiled, uttering a gasp. The crimp fell to the ground.

"Hey, I think I got a shock!" exclaimed Max. He gazed down at his fingers and frowned.

Me too, replied Lindsey silently, equally confused. She

picked up the crimp. It felt cold and lifeless between her fingers. "Strange," she muttered.

Under Max's watchful eye, she attached the crimp and swivel as he had shown her, and then placed the hook.

"Good." He raised his brows appraisingly. "You're a natural, Lindsey." He picked up his rod. "Well, let's get this show on the road."

Lindsey gazed at the boat nervously, watching him step in and balance himself with ease. He shrugged off his rucksack. "Hand me my tackle box, will you?"

He took it from her and set it under the seat. She handed him the rods, the cooler, and her knapsack.

"Okay. Now you."

Lindsey hesitated, shifting her gaze form the water to the boat and to his outstretched hand.

He waited for a patient moment. "Unless you'd like to fish by correspondence?"

Lindsey drew in a breath and clasped his hand, cautiously moving her foot to the side of the boat.

"In you go!" With a swift motion he gripped her hips and swung her down. The boat rocked precariously from side to side, and Lindsey fell against him.

Max steadied her, grinning at her startled expression. "Takes a moment to get your sea legs," he said wryly.

"I-I'm not much of a sailor," she admitted, recovering herself. She sat down opposite him, struggling to calm the jitters in her stomach, and managed to return his smile. *You can do this, Lindsey.*

But as he started the motor and sputtered out across the water, her stomach sprang up into her throat, and she clung to the sides of the boat.

"You have to learn how to read the water," he shouted over the roar of the motor. "Last weekend when we were here, we found a great place over there—downstream by those weedbeds." He pointed over her head.

We? You were here with Charlene? Lindsey gazed behind her as they passed through a bend in the river, idling slowly past overhanging bankside trees and plants.

"Weed beds attract a lot of animal life for the fish to feed on," he told her. "And it's a nice place for them to hide out—"

He stopped short as they spied the other boat. Two elderly men were sitting back to back, casting their lines. They glanced over at Max and Lindsey, barely acknowledging them, and returned to their fishing.

Max clenched his jaw and swung the boat around. "I guess someone else had the same idea," he said irritably.

"Can't we share the spot?" said Lindsly.

Max stared at her, his eyes seeming to penetrate hers. "I was hoping for some privacy."

Lindsey was getting used to the motion of the boat. The tension began to ebb from her shoulders, and she could feel her muscles slacken a little. She turned her face up toward the sun, enjoying the warmth on her skin. The rhythmic lapping of the water against the sides of the boat slowed her heartbeat, lulling her with it. She closed her eyes, drifting, dozing for a moment as she leaned back.

"Wakey, wakey." Max prodded her knee gently.

Lindsey blinked, sitting up with a start. "Oh, I must've dozed off."

They were floating on the water, and Max had his hook in his hand, already baited with a wriggling worm. Lindsey gazed about them. Off in the distance, she could make out only part of the boat dock.

"We're far away from home," said Max, following her gaze. He tossed her a life jacket. "Here. You better put that on. You look a little nervous."

"I'm not nervous," she retorted, but slipped on the life jacket, anyway. What she'd forgotten to tell him was that she couldn't swim—no, that wasn't true; she could dog paddle a little.

The Electric Cupid

"It's just you and me and the fish," he said, handing her a small tin can, "and the bait."

Lindsey stared at the worms squirming and writhing inside the tin. "Er . . ." She swallowed, pursing her lips together with a shuddering wince.

"Or would you prefer maggots?" He held up another can.

Lindsey wrinkled her nose, fighting to keep the color in her face. "Don't—don't you have anything else?" *That's not alive?* she wanted to add.

Max let out a low laugh and donned a khaki cap that matched his vest. "I never pegged you for the squeamish type—ah, but then, you're also afraid of dentists, aren't you?" His hazel-brown eyes twinkled beneath his cap. He reached into one of his pockets and extracted a rumpled hat. "You forgot your hat. Put this on." He tossed it to her. "I don't want you passing out on me."

I'm going to pass out if I have to keep looking at these worms, she thought, shoving the can out of her view.

"Here. I'll show you." Max hunkered down before her, and picked up her rod.

"You have to hook it twice, top and bottom, so it won't fly off when you cast," he said, looking at her. "And you want the fish to take the bait and the hook, not just tear off the worm."

Lindsey nodded squeamishly.

"There." He returned to his seat. "Now we cast the line."

He showed her again how to grip, with thumb and forefinger together. "The thumb runs along the top of the hand, like this."

Together they wound the float to about a yard from the rod tip as they had practiced at the boat dock.

"Remember, open the bail arm and press the line against the spool with your index finger. Then bring the rod back over the shoulder, and punch forward over your head—"

"I remember," said Lindsey impatiently.

"Okay, let's see you do it." He smiled.

"You first."

Max cast his line, the floater describing a perfect backward arc above his head, then climbing forward into the water.

Lindsey chewed on her lip, concentrating. It really wasn't all that difficult, she decided.

She imitated his movement, only as she brought the rod forward she forgot to release the line. The worm dangled inches above the water.

"You have to release—"

"I know, I know," she interrupted, irritated.

She cast again. And again the worm hung there on the end of her rod.

"You feeling sorry for the worm?" Max grinned, tilting his head at her. "Or are you just waiting for the fish to jump up and grab the bait?"

Lindsey suppressed her embarrassment with a withering look. "I'm just practicing," she grumbled.

Her third attempt at casting landed her line in a jumbled heap on the water. Without looking at him, she reeled in the line.

Max said nothing, but watched her out of the corner of her eye, a wry grin on his face.

It was on her sixth unsuccessful casting attempt that Lindsey finally sat back, annoyed and defeated. She gazed at Max, waiting for his comment.

"You'll get it," was all he said.

She wondered if Charlene ever had any trouble casting. Her expression soured; probably not. She sighed. "Maybe, er, you could . . ." Her words faltered.

Max turned his head, squinting at her. "You asking for my help, Lindsey McGinty?"

Lindsey rolled her eyes. "Yes," she said reluctantly.

But he merely returned his gaze to his own line, not

moving. "You're releasing the line too early. Try following the path of the rod tip until the rod is horizontal. You're also aiming too low, and you need more power on the forward punch."

Lindsey mulled over this advice, hesitating. Maybe this fishing business just wasn't her bag. She was much better at land sports: tennis, golf, baseball. But fishing—well, maybe this was a man's sport after all.

"It took me a week before I could cast properly," said Max, jarring her from her thoughts. "Just keep trying. You'll get it."

Lindsey exhaled a loud sigh. *Here goes.*

She followed the rod back and punched forward, releasing the line. The float sunk in the water, then bobbed to the surface. Her frown metamorphosed into a proud grin.

"Not bad," said Max, nodding at her. "But maybe you didn't notice—your worm is somewhere behind us."

Lindsey groaned. "Maybe I'll get lucky?"

"That hook is attractive, but not that attractive," said Max, his lips turning up into a teasing smile. "A fish is not that different from a man, really. A pretty shell only holds so much allure. There has to be a little more to... you know, hold a man's interest."

Lindsey cocked an eyebrow. "And what exactly constitutes 'a little more'?"

Max's teeth flashed at her. "Electricity."

Lindsey nearly dropped her fishing pole into the river.

Chapter Eight

The sun was now directly overhead, beating down on them, making the perspiration run down Lindsey's back and under her arms. Her eyelids drooped sleepily as she stared, as if mesmerized, at the red-and-white float. The life jacket over her sweatshirt was a suit of armor, sapping the energy from her body. She thought how she might slip off her sweatshirt without letting go of her rod.

"Yah! Gotcha!" Max suddenly pulled back on his rod, slowing the spool with his finger.

Lindsey heard the mosquito sound of the reel backwinding, and glanced over at him.

"Whoa! This one's feisty!" He bobbed the rod and engaged the anti-reverse on the reel. The boat rocked as he half-stood, gripping the rod with both hands. "Lindsey! Get the net, will you?"

The afternoon's fuzziness suddenly drew back, like a curtain being thrust open across her head, and her muscles creaked alive. These were the first words he'd spoken to her in what seemed hours. She awkwardly bent over the tackle box and snatched up the net with her free hand.

"I'm tiring him. Get ready," Max instructed.

Lindsey kicked aside the rucksack that slid toward her and straddled the tackle box. "Er—" She glanced back at her other hand which was still holding her own reel.

Max rapidly reeled in the line. "You have to get closer! Get under it."

"I, er—" She stretched as far as she could go, now with one foot planted at each end of the boat.

The head of the fish surfaced, then the long torpedo-shaped body. It twitched convulsively, fighting an invisible enemy.

"Get the net under him!" Max struggled to control the line. "Hurry! I'm going to lose him!"

As Lindsey reached out with the net, the boat tipped and jerked under her weight. Unable to keep her balance, the fishing rod slipped from her hand, and she felt herself fly sprawling over the edge. The side of the boat rammed into her stomach and she let out a wailing "Oof!"

But still her hand clenched the handle of the net.

"Got him!" shouted Max as the torpedo-shaped body folded, still twitching, into the net. "Okay, Lindsey. Bring him in."

"Er, maybe you could . . ." Lindsey grunted, now forced to hold onto the net with both hands. She eyed the water that loomed closer as the weight of the fish tipped her body dangerously forward.

She felt his hand grab the waist of her jeans and tug her back into the boat. "Don't worry. I gotcha."

Lindsey's muscles strained as she heaved in the net. The mottled brown fish was still convulsing, but with less conviction, its earlier energy now slowly waning.

"Way to go, partner!" Max slapped her on the shoulder. Lindsey stumbled forward. "See? We do make a great team!"

Lindsey glanced over at her side of the boat, grimacing. Her fishing pole wasn't there.

"Er, Max? I think I drop—"

"A northern pike," observed Max. "And one of the biggest I've seen in a long time. He must weigh at least twenty, maybe twenty-five pounds. And a fighter. You held onto that net like a real trouper, Lindsey." He deftly removed the hook from the pike's mouth, gently picked up the torpedo body, and leaned over the side of the boat where he let him go.

"What—?"

Max ran his fingers around the bill of his cap and grinned. "Ah, there he goes. An old general with another notch under his fins."

Lindsey looked at him, baffled, then suddenly remembered her fishing pole. "My pole!" She scrambled to the other side of the boat, which rocked precariously from side to side.

She saw it, sinking slowly under the weight of the reel. Leaning over the side of the boat, she reached for it. Just a little more . . . Her fingers dipped into the water, grazing the graphite pole, but still unable to grapple a firm hold. She inched farther so that the boat edge dug into her upper thighs. Her hand closed over the handle.

"Got it!"

She heard Max call out her name just as she felt a wave of water lap over her head. But before she could recover herself, she was already falling, stunned for an instant by the sudden cold that swallowed her. She flailed, paddling up for air, and gasped as she buoyed back to the surface.

Max's grinning face looked down on her. "You competing with the fishies now? Tell me what kind of bait you prefer and I'll get my hook ready."

Lindsey glowered up at him. Her fingers, she noticed, were still gripping the handle of the fishing pole. "Your hand will do," she growled, throwing the rod over into the boat.

Stupid fishing pole. Stupid fish. What am I doing here, anyway? I'm not a fisherman . . . a fisherwoman . . . fisherperson—aaah, whatever, she grumbled to herself.

"You know, it's going to be a little tough trying to fish from down there. For one, you don't look like a fish, and you're making an awful racket splashing around like that—"

She clasped his hand, and for a moment was tempted to pull him and his smug grin into the water with her.

But his grip was steady, warm, reassuring, and Lindsey found herself at once welcoming his help, relaxing into his strong arms as they fastened around her waist, holding her close. Max helped her regain her balance, his eyes gazing at her with concern.

"Cold?" He didn't let go of her, but rather held her more tightly.

Lindsey realized then that she was shivering despite the hot sun, despite the warmth of his body pressed against hers.

"N-no." She shook her head, brushing the wet strands of hair from her eyes.

Max eyed her, rolling his lips between his teeth thoughtfully. He dropped his hands and squinted up at the sky. "It's about one, I'd guess. Maybe we'd better head back and get you out of those wet clothes."

Lindsey's heart drummed a sinking beat. She shook her head, spraying water about her. "No. I don't want to ruin— your day." *My day,* she'd almost said. "The sun will dry my clothes," she added with a quick smile.

"I almost forgot how tough you are," murmured Max. He sat down and pulled out his rucksack. "Let's see what I have in here."

Lindsey sat down heavily, unbelted the life jacket, and slipped it off. She wrung out the sleeves and front of her sweatshirt. Her jeans clung to her legs, the soaked material weighing down her limbs. She sighed, cringing as she replayed the clumsy scene in her mind. He must think her a total fool, she thought.

"Aha! Here we go." He unrolled a red checked shirt. "It might be a little big." He grinned at her, holding it up. "But at least it's dry." He tossed it to her and gazed at her wet jeans, frowning. "I can give you my pants, if you like."

"Your pants?" She watched him stand up and unfasten the bib straps of his fishing overalls and unzip the sides. "No, wait—"

But he already had them down, revealing tight-fitting jeans underneath. He uttered a low chuckle at her startled expression, taking an almost impish delight in the color that rose to her cheeks.

"Don't worry. I'm not an exhibitionist," he said teasingly. He glanced about him as he handed her the overalls. "Actually, there's no one around to see."

Lindsey snatched the fishing pants from him, but observed that he was right in his assessment of their situation; they'd drifted further downstream and the boat dock was now completely obscured by the jutting bank. The boat they'd encountered an hour ago had moved on and there was no one in sight.

She inspected the shirt. It was undoubtedly a man's shirt, and it smelled faintly musty. But it was clean.

"Well?" Max regarded her, eyebrows raised.

Lindsey gave him a long look, gesturing to him with her hand. "Turn around, please." *You're my dentist, not my doctor,* she muttered tartly to herself. But the way he looked at her made her heartbeat quicken, and her gaze blackened.

He smiled, shrugged, then obeyed. He picked up his fishing rod and proceded to cast with his back facing her.

She kept her eyes on him as she peeled off her wet sweatshirt and T-shirt. With a quick motion she donned the checked shirt, buttoned it, and rolled up the sleeves to her wrists. She wrenched off her sneakers and socks, draping them alongside her other wet things.

The jeans proved to be more difficult, and as she tried to wrest them off, she lost her balance, causing the boat to sway and dip.

"You need a hand?" Max half-turned.

"Just keep your eyes where they are," commanded Lindsey, stifling a grunt.

"Because you know, if you fall in again—"

"Don't worry about me. I've been dressing myself since I was three." *But this is the first time I've changed clothes on a boat,* she thought, finally managing to free her other foot from the pantleg. She regarded the bibbed overalls doubtfully, but proceded to climb into them.

"Hey! You hungry?" he called over after a moment.

Lindsey was busy trying to adjust the bib straps.

"You look like a real fisherman, now—or rather, uh, fisherwoman—"

"Angler," she cut in, tugging at the braces in frustration.

Max set down his pole and moved gracefully toward her, his steps steadying the motion of the boat rather than rocking it. He squatted down before her and moved her hands away from the bib braces.

"It's a little tricky," he murmured, and with deft fingers he tightened the left strap. Wordlessly, he adjusted the other side to match. "Good?"

Lindsey nodded, meeting his gaze then immediately glancing away. She compressed her lips to keep herself from flushing, hoping he couldn't hear the brass band banging away in her chest. What was wrong with her? Darn it! Why did she feel so giddy all of a sudden?

"You okay?" He was gazing at her curiously, his straight brows locked together in concern.

"I-I'm just hungry," she said, forcing her lips into a smile.

"After that little swim, I don't doubt it." He grinned. He slid out the cooler from beneath her seat and handed her a root beer.

"I'm sorry. I know you like juice. I—I didn't get around to doing any shopping this week," she apologized.

"Juice? Oh, actually I prefer root beer," he said, extracting one for himself. "It's Charlene who drinks juice." He handed her a sandwich. "It's chicken salad, I think. Charlene made them for us last night."

Oh? Charlene helps you decorate your house, buys your groceries, cooks for you—indispensable, isn't she? wondered Lindsey.

And as if translating her thoughts, Max sat down opposite her and sighed. "Charlene's been a great help these past couple of months. I don't know what I'd do without her."

"Learn how to cook on your own, maybe?" muttered Lindsey. And realizing she'd uttered this thought aloud, she quickly bit into the sandwich.

The chicken salad melted in her mouth, and Lindsey admitted, with some reluctance, that the sandwich was delicious—with just the right amount of seasoning and mayonnaise mixture to satisfy her palate. She'd almost hoped that it would taste awful, that beautiful, porcelain-skinned Charlene was more of a failure in the kitchen than Lindsey.

"It's true, I admit it," Max interrupted her thoughts, "that I've been somewhat spoiled, growing up with three doting sisters," he said between chews. "And I guess it doesn't help that I'm the youngest, either. They certainly weren't thrilled with the idea of their baby brother moving here to big bad Boston."

"Do you miss Saint Andrews?"

Max took off his cap and rubbed his forehead, gazing out across the river. "Yes, I guess I do." He sighed, smiling wistfully. "But—" He donned his cap again, his eyes shifting back to her. "This city's growing on me—Hey! your hat."

Lindsey's hand went to her bare head, her short hair already beginning to dry in the afternoon sun. "Oh, no! I think I might've lost it when I fell in."

"No, here it is." Max scooped up the hat wedged between the tackle box and the rucksack. He threw it onto her lap. "I'd advise you to put it on. Charlene got sunstroke once when we were out on Passamaquoddy Bay. Her hat got snagged in a tree and she refused to wear that one." He snorted. "Said it smelled funny. She's a little finicky when it comes to things like that."

Lindsey sniffed the hat. It smelled like the sea—and *him*—with that tantalizing, musky odor seeming to pervade everything he touched. She put it on, noting the smile that played on his lips as he watched her. His intent gaze made her heart flutter a little and she flushed.

A beat of silence passed between them, and Lindsey found herself searching for something to say, anything—

"Sun's hot," she suddenly blurted, and immediately shrank away from the inanity of the remark. *He must think you incredibly dull,* she groaned inwardly.

Max leaned forward and rested his elbows on his thighs, folding his hands together under his chin. "So, Lindsey McGinty. Why don't you tell me about yourself? I mean, what do you do besides install new electrical panels and put up high-hat lights?"

Lindsey shrugged. "Hmmm . . . well—" she stammered. She wasn't used to men asking her to talk about herself. Center stage was normally reserved for her dates, with her being stuck down in the audience listening to them prattle on self-importantly about themselves and their work.

And so it was with much guardedness, mingled with a sudden onset of shyness, that Lindsey began to speak. But as Max tilted his head and listened without interruption, nodding his head intermittently, Lindsey found herself chattering away easily. Words rushed out of her, and before she could stop herself she realized she was spilling out— sharing with this man—some of her more intimate thoughts.

After a few minutes, she suddenly paused, self-consciously aware she was dominating the conversation, that he'd allowed her to prattle on about herself.

"You're not used to talking about yourself, are you?" he observed with a small smile.

Please, stop looking at me that way, she pleaded silently. *You're going to make me fall in love with you.*

"I just get tired of hearing my own voice, that's all," she said, shrugging. "How about you take a turn? I'd really like to hear about New Brunswick—about Saint Andrews."

Tell me about you and Charlene, she added silently. *Do you often take her fishing with you? If she left Boston, would you follow her back to Saint Andrews? Is she still the love of your life, Max? Do you still love her the way you did in high school? The way you did that night when you took her to the prom?*

All these questions she fired at him wordlessly through her eyes, her fingers absently twisting the buckles on the bibbed pants, watching him, waiting for him to speak.

But Max's attention was instantly diverted by a sudden call that sounded behind her. Lindsey shifted in the bench seat and turned her head.

"Hey—ho! Greetings, fellow sailors! We hate to intrude—"

"Lenny?" Lindsey blinked incredulously, squinting at him with one eye.

"Why, I'll be! Is that who I think it is? Lindsey?" An expression of mock astonishment broke across his face. "I can't believe this. What a coincidence!"

Lindsey rolled her eyes and stifled the groan in her throat. Lenny wasn't fooling anybody; he knew darn well she'd be here with Max. Her neighbor's transparency was one thing Lindsey could always count on; Lenny was easier to read than the giant billboards along the freeway.

But what was he doing here? she wondered.

Lindsey then spied Lenny's companion. His date smiled affably at them, apparently unperturbed by this "coincidental" meeting. Indeed, the woman reminded Lindsey of a cat dozing on a windowsill, with eyes half-closed, mouth turned up in a contented lazy smile, her back resting comfortably against the protruding rib of the boat.

Lenny and Max were exchanging words, Max smiling out of the side of his mouth as he offered Lindsey's neighbor some advice. From Lenny's attire—hatless, with a black leather vest (one of his "Sunday bests," Lindsey noted) slung over a long-sleeved white shirt, black dress trousers hiked up to reveal black and silver cowboy boots—it was evident to both Max and Lindsey he didn't know the first thing about fishing.

"Miranda Caulfield, this is Lindsey McGinty, my upstairs neighbor," introduced Lenny, his normal leering smile too wide, his nervousness showing in the sweat that dampened his brow and upper lip. "And this is her, uh, dentist, Max Rupert."

"Hi." Miranda waved. Her peroxided hair was a shade too brassy, her makeup clownishly colorful, and she wore a scoop-necked red T-shirt that seemed to lump together, rather than accentuate, the ample curves of her figure. But there was a friendly ease about this woman, a savvy, good-humored look behind those blue-shadowed eyes, and Lindsey found herself taking an instant liking to her.

". . . this was Miranda's idea," Lenny rushed on breathlessly, taking in Lindsey's inquiring glance.

"I'm from Maine, you see. My mother's a champion surf caster, and my pop's a fisherman by trade," said Miranda. She smiled at Lenny. "I thought I'd show this guy a few tricks of the trade."

Lindsey regarded her neighbor, and was almost more astonished than amused by the self-conscious blush that seeped up his burly neck, turning his face and ears scarlet. He coughed, and shot a quick glance in Lindsey's direction, the look on his face crying out, *"Help me; I'm drowning!"*

But it was Max who came to his rescue.

"Well, you're welcome to share our spot, if you like." He nodded to Lenny.

Miranda gazed up at the sun and reached for a pair of leopard-spotted sunglasses. "I was thinking we'd make our way over to that shaded area. Looks like a nice feeding spot." She pointed to the bank of overhanging trees and weed beds, Max and Lindsey's original destination.

"Besides, you two look like you'd like some privacy," Miranda added.

Behind those dark leopard-spotted glasses, Lindsey couldn't tell who Miranda was gazing at, but her meaningful smile said enough.

However, it was Lenny who shifted nervously in the boat, his ears now surpassing the color of Miranda's shirt.

"You have enough bait, then?" said Max.

Miranda's smile was slow, her red-lipsticked lips stretching across large white teeth. "Oh, yes. I have enough bait."

Lenny kneaded his hands together nervously.

Max and Lindsey watched them roar away, two unlikely looking anglers out on their first date. Lindsey chuckled under her breath, recalling Lenny's parting expression: *"Now what do I do?"* he'd telegraphed to her in silent anxiety.

"An interesting couple," remarked Max, opening his tackle box. He fished out the tin can of bait.

"I've never seen Lenny so nervous," said Lindsey.

"Love can do that to people. It can make you a nervous wreck."

Lindsey gave him a sidelong look, taking the opportunity to study him as he hooked a wriggling maggot on the end of his line.

"She's . . . interesting," said Lindsey. "Not exactly what I pictured. But I think—"

"Don't tell me you're jealous." Max glanced up at her from beneath his cap.

Jealous? The thought was so ridiculous she almost laughed aloud. "What I was going to say was that I think it's nice Lenny finally found someone. I mean, she's perfect for him."

"You believe that, then?"

"What do you mean? Believe what?"

"That there are people who are perfect for each other."

Lindsey thought about this for a moment. "I don't know. At one time I think I would've answered: 'definitely not.' But now?" She shrugged. "I don't know. My friend Rhonda believes that there is someone out there for everyone. You just have to—" Lindsey exhaled and rolled up the sleeves of her shirt further as hot sweat trickled down the small of her back.

"Have faith?" ventured Max, finishing her sentence.

"You just have to keep looking," corrected Lindsey.

"But sometimes we can get so caught up in the search, we miss what's right there in front of us." His hazel-brown eyes sought out hers, his gaze holding her for a long moment until he turned his head and returned his attention to his hook.

Something leaped in Lindsey's chest. Her ears began to pound. The chicken salad sandwiches churned in her stomach, and Lindsey bit her lip as a sudden wave of dizziness washed over her.

"Maggot, or worm?"

Lindsey's hand went to her stomach. "Excuse me?"

"Hmmm . . . you want me to bait your hook for you again?" He grinned at her. "Not everyone has the stomach for—"

Lindsey pursed her lips, and snatched the can from him. She swallowed as she eyed the white caterpillarlike things squirming around on top of each other. "No," she said firmly. "I can do it."

"I wonder what Miranda and Lenny are using for bait?" mused Max, reeling out his line.

Lindsey suppressed a grin as an image of Lenny, with his cowhide boots and leather vest, loomed in her mind.

She glanced over toward the jutting bank, but her downstairs neighbor and his date were camouflaged by the swarm of trees and plants.

Yes, there's someone out there for everyone—even for Lenny, she thought.

She turned to watch Max cast his line.

Between forefinger and thumb she held up a maggot, and wrinkled her nose.

You just have to have the right bait, she added with a grimace.

"Well, now we know what interests these fish," said Max, watching Lindsey's second catch of the day swim away.

Maggots, thought Lindsey with a small shudder.

"I'll make a fisherman—excuse me, *angler*—of you yet," said Max, rubbing his neck.

"Do you ever keep any of the fish you catch?" Her eyes burned a little as they adjusted to the dusky light falling about them. The river took on a pinkish gray twinkle, and a breeze waded in from the east, stirring the boat into a gentle rock.

"Not since last summer when I caught the Admiral."

"The Admiral?"

Max nodded. "Ol' Wily Wilbur."

"Wily Wilbur. You mean the fish your nephew said he caught?"

"Uh-huh. A magnificent king carp. Wears his scales like a suit of leather armor. Moves like a professional boxer in the water, duking his eighty-pound body around fisherman's lines, feinting left, then right—then just *poof!* disappearing." Max stroked the cleft in his chin, chuckling softly. "If you study him, you can almost see his strategy at play. You think you're hunting him, but really, it's he who's watching you play *his* game, working yourself into a frustrated frenzy."

Lindsey heard the awe in his voice. "But you managed to catch him."

Max laughed. "Uh-huh. With a piece of cheese."

"Cheese?"

He shook his head. "For four and a half hours, he'd been circling, lunging at every bait I put on my hook. Finally, I ran out of all of my live bait. I had nothing left. But I was determined to catch that ol' guy, so in a last desperate attempt, I hooked on a hunk of cheese."

"And he went for it?"

"Hook, line, and sinker."

"But you let him go."

"Yup." Matt nodded. He removed his cap and ran his hand through his hair. "Funny thing. There he was, this beautiful magnificent fish, thrashing around in my net. I thought to myself: 'This is the Admiral you've caught, Max; for years you've been trying to snag ol' Wily Wilbur.'" He exhaled loudly, pausing for a moment to gaze out at the river.

"There he was in my net. I'd caught him! I should have been jubilant. I mean, it was a fisherman's dream—catching ol' Wily Wilbur! But then—" He suddenly turned to Lindsey, his face reflecting the silvery pink shimmers of the water. "One second, I had him—and the next, I was throwing him back into the bay. Don't ask me why I did it, because I don't know myself. I just knew he didn't belong with me." His eyes turned from the river, falling to his fishing rod which he began to disassemble.

Lindsey sat watching him, quietly listening to the steady rhythm of the water lap up against the sides of the boat. They said nothing for a long while, even as the sun sank behind the trees like a weary eye.

"So, why did you decide to—"

"Maybe we'd better—"

They laughed as their voices melded together, slicing

through the quiet. A lone gull squawked overhead at them as if to say, "What are you two still doing here?"

"Ladies first," said Max.

Lindsey shrugged. She had been about to ask him why he'd decided to leave Saint Andrews, but the question seemed irrelevant now. And it was getting late. She still had things to do—water Rhonda's plants, for starters.

"Maybe it's time we started heading back," she said.

Max agreed. "You have any plans for dinner?"

"I was going to defrost some fish sticks," she said with a low laugh. "But I think I'm all fished out."

He chuckled, snapping on the lids of the bait tins. "I wonder how Lenny and Miranda are making out," he mused, gazing westward toward the cover of trees, now enshrouded in twilit shadow.

"Hmmm . . . they still haven't come out yet. Maybe we should go over there—"

"I wouldn't worry. I have a feeling Miranda knows what she's doing," Max cut in. There was a hint of amusement in his voice. "She's certainly equipped."

Lindsey shot him a harsh look out of the corner of her eye.

"I'm talking about her Plano 757."

Lindsey looked at him. His teeth gleamed whitely even in the graying light, and in his eyes were reflected the twinklets of silvery-pink that shimmered all along the surface of the river.

"Plano 757?" she inquired. What was he talking about?

"Plano 757. One of the best—certainly the largest, most durable tackle boxes on the market," said Max. "Looked like a hardwood antique, too—aluminum waterproofed, metal hinges. Beautiful."

"Well, I guess Lenny's in . . . good hands, then," said Lindsey, collecting her clothes which were dry, but stiff. Her sweatshirt and T-shirt had taken on the shape of the boat's ribbed bottom, and her jeans put up a rigid resistance as she tried to fold them up and shove them into her knapsack.

"So, you know any restaurants around here?" Max asked her, starting up the motor.

Lindsey glanced down at the borrowed bibbed fishing overalls she was wearing, her hand going to her head, not wanting to think about what her hair looked like underneath her hat. "You mean . . . go eat, now? Like this?"

"Sure. Why not?" He cocked his head, his expression suddenly inscrutable as clouds congregated above them, moving together, pausing just overhead as if to eavesdrop on their conversation.

"You look fine to me," he added with a slow grin.

Lindsey's blush melded with the shadows of the approaching evening. Was he flirting with her? Or just teasing—baiting her? For she sensed in his words almost a jesting quality—the way he grinned at her beneath his cap, the gleam of mischief she'd glimpsed in his eyes.

Lindsey squeezed out these interpretive musings from her mind and regarded him with irritation. "I really have a lot of things to do," she shouted over the motor's roar. She glanced down at her watch—her *nonwaterproof* watch. The little hand pointed to the one, the big hand to the five.

"Aw, gee—" She suppressed a curse, and gritted her teeth together hard. This action sent a jolt of pain up along the base of her left jaw. Before she could cover her mouth, she let out a loud yelp.

Max heard it over the sound of the motor, and swiftly cut it. "Hey, you okay? Your teeth bothering you?" The boat swayed as he moved toward her. "Maybe I should take a look—"

"No, no. Sit down. I'm fine," she assured him, waving him back.

The grin that broke across his face was so unsubtle, so boyish, that Lindsey found herself grinning back at him.

"Oh, I can see you're fine." He sat down, restarted the

motor, and steered them toward the boat docks. "How about Italian?" he shouted.

Lindsey thought about the big pot of leftover spaghetti sauce shoved to the back of her fridge. Like all her other leftovers it would stagnate there for weeks—at least until she felt like cooking again, and then, of course, it would have spoiled.

Should she invite him over?

"Er, Max? Why don't you come over to . . . my place?"

"What's that?" Max cupped his ear, frowning at the boat engine whose whiny roar seemed to fill the river and the entire park beyond.

Lindsey winced. *What if he says no?* She immediately snorted at herself. *You mean, what if he says yes. Don't you remember what state the apartment was in when you left it this morning? No, you can't invite him into that pigsty,* decided Lindsey. *At least, not yet.*

But Lindsey recognized this as just another excuse, another way of avoiding getting too involved with Max. What was she afraid of? Did she think she might actually fall head over heels in love with this man?

They coasted into the docks, and Max helped her out of the boat.

"Sorry," he said, "Couldn't hear you over that darn motor. What was the name of that restaurant again?"

Chez Lindsey, she replied silently.

She looked down at her clothes. "Maybe it's not such a good idea. I mean, I can't go anywhere looking like this—" She suddenly remembered Rhonda's instructions. "Oh! I almost forgot. I have to water my friend Rhonda's plants. So maybe you'd better drive me home, and then I'll go over to Rhonda's—"

"I'll drive you to Rhonda's," said Max, shouldering his rucksack. He picked up his tackle box. He closed his hand over the two fishing poles, and made his way up to the dark sloping path where his Chevrolet was parked.

The Electric Cupid

Lindsey put her arms through the straps of her knapsack and hefted the cooler. She was tired, excited, apprehensive. After a brief reflective pause, she turned toward the path and followed Max.

"And then, we'll head over to your place," he called over his shoulder. "Say, Lindsey, you wouldn't happen to have any spaghetti at your place, would you? Hmmm... I haven't had a good spaghetti dinner in a long time."

"Yeah, me neither," lied Lindsey. *Not my place*, she thought with a grimace. And she decided then that she didn't really look all that bad, that after she finished watering Rhonda's plants she'd let Max take her out to dinner.

"Of course we could go out for dinner," said Max, unlocking the trunk.

"You read my mind," mumbled Lindsey.

"Italian, okay?"

"Well—all right."

He reached for the cooler.

"I can handle it," she said, opening the back door and sliding in the cooler. But before she could round her way over to the front passenger side, Max was there holding it open for her.

"So it's settled. I'll take you out to dinner." He grinned at her stiffening reaction, and tapped the bill of his cap in a gesture of mock chivalry. "Of course, mademoiselle, if you prefer, you can always pick up the check."

Chapter Nine

Lindsey was rummaging inside her knapsack, muttering to herself and squinting under the car's pale interior light. "I'll just be a moment," she assured him, pulling out her stiff T-shirt and sweatshirt. Why hadn't she cleaned this thing out before she left?

After a few moments of watching her frantic searching, Max cleared his throat, interrupting her muttering. "What exactly are you looking for?"

"Rhonda's key—*my* keys, actually—" Lindsey's hand froze in the air, her face suddenly very still. She snapped her fingers, remembering. "My jeans pocket! I put them in the front left pocket—" She yanked out the still-damp jeans, unrolled them, and thrust her fingers in both front pockets.

She bit her lip and cringed. "Uh-oh."

"Your keys—they're not in your pockets?"

Lindsey glanced at him. "No. But I think I know where I can find them." She sighed glumly, her shoulders slumping forward.

Max mirrored her grimace. "You don't mean—"

"Good thing fish can't drive." She groaned, massaging her temples.

"Well, does Rhonda have another extra key lying around?" suggested Max. "Like under the front doormat, or maybe in the flower pot?"

Lindsey shot him a look of incredulity. "This isn't Saint

Andrews, Max. You can't just leave keys lying outside the house."

"Hmmm... yes. Charlene lectured me about the same thing just the other day. She thinks I'm too trusting."

When it comes to that woman, you are, thought Lindsey.

"Well, you must have another set of keys at home, right?" he said.

"Actually, yes. I do have another set of keys."

Max started the car. "I'll take you home, then."

"Unfortunately, that won't do any good."

Max's hand paused on the gearshift. "What do you mean?"

"My extra set of keys aren't at my apartment."

"Oh? Where are they, then?"

Lindsey pointed at Rhonda's house, wincing. "In there."

Max grunted, his face reddening with exertion as Lindsey raised herself from his clasped hands and gripped the ledge of the windowsill.

"I thought you said Lenny's got a spare key. So why—"

"A spare key to the *house*, not my truck or my locker at work—hold steady. Okay, just a little more—" She swung her knee up on the ledge and pulled herself up.

"I still think we should call a locksmith," puffed Max.

"It's all right. You see, it's a trick window. Rhonda and I had to do this a couple of years ago when Rick was in Washington and she locked herself out of the house."

"Be careful," said Max, spotlighting her with his flashlight.

Lindsey squinted and shaded her eyes. "Get that thing out of my face." The beam lowered as she rattled the screen. But it did not budge. She tried the other end. It, too, was stuck tight.

"Shine the light on the hinges over here," she instructed. "Hmmm... now that I think of it, I don't actually remember there ever being a screen on this window—hey! You trying to blind me? Shine that thing on the *window,* not *me*—"

"You up there! Stop what you're doing and come down from that ledge!"

Lindsey froze, staring transfixedly into the beam of light.

The policeman behind the light shifted to his other foot, his patience visibly waning. "All right, now! Get down from there—and keep your hands where I can see them!"

"Maybe I should help her down?" came Max's voice from the adjacent shadows.

"You stay where you are!" growled the policeman. "All right! You up there! You need any help?"

But Lindsey was already slipping herself down as soon as she'd heard Max's voice. She dangled from the ledge for a moment, then leaped to the ground. Did Max think she was actually scared to jump down? thought Lindsey with a derisive snort. And just because she was a woman didn't mean she needed help—

"Against the wall, both of you," ordered the policeman, gesturing with his flashlight. Lindsey noted thankfully that the officer hadn't seen any need to draw his weapon.

"Hands on the wall, ma'am," he instructed.

Lindsey looked at Max, who was staring back at her. The incredulous look on both their faces made them smile. A giggle threatened to bubble up from Lindsey's throat, and she bit her lip, swallowing.

"Er, officer? My name is Lindsey McGinty. I am looking after my friend's house while she and her husband are in Hawaii," she explained quickly.

The policeman was glancing through Max's wallet. "You have any ID, ma'am?"

Lindsey winced; she hadn't thought to bring her wallet with her. "Er, yes. At my apartment. You see, we couldn't get in to water Rhonda's plants—"

"Your friend didn't bother to leave you a key?" The officer's tone was skeptical.

"She lost the key while we were fishing in Stony Brook River today."

"You two are married?"

"No, we're, uh—" Max cast a glance at Lindsey. "I'm ... her dentist."

"Look, officer, if you want, you can ask Madame Snoop—I, er, mean, Mrs. Olafson. The next-door neighbor—she knows me," said Lindsey.

"It was Mrs. Olafson who made the complaint. She said she saw two suspicious-looking characters skulking arund the back of this house."

Suspicious-looking? Lindsey exhaled a loud sigh of frustration. "We're not trying to rob the place. I just have to get in to water Rhonda's plants and get my spare set of keys."

"Is there anyone who can corroborate your story?" The officer sounded tired.

Lindsey couldn't think of anyone, and so they all ended up trooping across Mrs. Olafson's lawn and knocking on her front door.

But Madame Snoop—Mrs. Olafson—could not be enticed to answer the door.

"Mrs. Olafson!" Lindsey called through the door, knowing that the elderly woman was standing on the opposite side, her ear pressed hard against the wood. "It's me, Mrs. Olafson: Lindsey McGinty. Rhonda's friend?"

"Rhonda who?"

"Rhonda Tierney, Mrs. Olafson. Your next-door neighbor."

"You're not Rhonda. Rhonda and her husband are in Hawaii."

"Yes, I know. I'm *Lindsey*—Rhonda's friend. You might've seen me around here with her." Lindsey knew for a fact Madame Snoop had seen her; she doubted there were any goings-on in this neighborhood that Mrs. Olafson wasn't aware of.

"Ma'am? Would you like to open you door and help us clear up this situation?" said the officer wearily. "You can keep the latch on, if you like," he assured her.

A moment passed. Max and Lindsey exchanged concerned looks, but underneath, they were both making valiant efforts to quash the giddy giggles that were threatening to surface.

Finally, Mrs. Olafson drew back the bolts and locks, and peered at them over the chain latch.

"Your identification," she ordered, narrowing her eyes at the policeman on her doorstep.

The officer sighed and flipped his badge at her. The Watchful Widow scrutinized it, then took a long look at the officer. She closed the door, and they could hear her removing the chain latch.

"Do you know these people?" asked the officer.

Mrs. Olafson's narrowed gray eyes swept over Lindsey, frowning. Lindsey followed her gaze and took in her own attire, suddenly aware of how odd she must look. She took off her cap and fluffed up her hair with her fingers—not that it helped.

But Mrs. Olafson's eyes suddenly lit up as her gaze fell to Max.

"Why, Dr. Rupert!" she exclaimed.

"You know this man, ma'am?"

The Watchful Widow nodded. "Dr. Rupert is my dentist. Fixed my false plate. Did a wonderful job, too."

"Hello, Mrs. Olafson." Max grinned. "Now, don't forget about your next appointment—"

"Mrs. Olafson. You know me—Lindsey McGinty?" Lindsey cut in.

Mrs. Olafson studied her for a long moment, tapping her chin with her finger. "Yes, now I recognize you. You're a friend of the Tierneys'. They're in Hawaii now," she said to the officer.

"Yes. I'm, er, supposed to be looking after the house,"

said Lindsey, hoping to jog the woman's memory. "To water the plants?"

"Yes. That's right. Wednesdays and Saturdays." Mrs. Olafson nodded.

Madame Snoop had been listening, all right, thought Lindsey.

"Sorry to bother you, Mrs. Olafson," said the officer belligerently. "I'll radio in a locksmith."

"Anything to help the police!" Mrs. Olafson called after him. She turned to Max. "Oh, Dr. Rupert? Please let Mrs. Honeysuckle know the caramel square recipe turned out perfectly. You'll thank her for me, won't you?"

"I will, Mrs. Olafson." Max nodded, avoiding Lindsey's sharp gaze.

"For a big city, you do manage to get around, Dr. Rupert," Lindsey muttered under her breath.

The officer had returned to his car and was speaking into the CB.

Max grinned at Lindsey. "Life is full of coincidences, isn't it?"

After the locksmith arrived, the officer gave them a brief lecture on prowling around after dark.

"I'd advise you two to leave the burglaring to professionals," he added sourly, and sped off.

"I thought we made a pretty good team," harrumphed Max.

Lindsey rubbed the back of her neck. "What a day." She sighed as the locksmith handed her the bill.

"The evening's just beginning," said Max, tramping after her into the house.

"So, you still feel like going out? That Thai restaurant we passed on the way over here looked interesting." Max moved about the living room, pausing to peruse the books on her shelves. He turned toward the reading floor lamp and reached his hand up under the shade to turn it on.

"Oh, don't bother with that. It doesn't work," said Lindsey.

Max's brows lifted. "Correct me if I'm wrong, but it seems a little odd—I mean, an electrician having electrical appliances that don't work."

Just don't ask for coffee, replied Lindsey silently, casting a weary glance at her rebellious coffee machine. "Well, I'm just going to slip into something a little more comfortable—" She stopped herself, not believing she'd just said that.

But Max was too busy, with head inclined quizzically to one side, scrutinizing a framed print on the far wall.

"That's a replica of—"

"Leyden's jar. Yes." Max nodded. He smiled at her look of surprise. "I know a little about . . . electricity."

Lindsey remembered the book she'd seen splayed out on his bed, and a slow flush burned into her face.

"Hey, we don't have to go out if you don't want to," said Max, fingering the cleft in his chin. He watched her with puzzled, interested eyes. "We could stay right here—order in a pizza, if you like."

Do I look that bad? she wondered, passing a self-conscious hand through her limp hair. She shrugged. "Sure. There's a place just around the corner from here. Just dial memory #3." Why did he have to look so attractive? And why was her heart suddenly doing aerobics?

Max reached for the phone on the coffee table. "What do you like on your pizza?"

Lindsey moved into the bedroom. "Anything's fine," she called out. Her stomach growled. "Whatever you want," she added quietly, shutting the door behind her.

She took a moment to catch her breath, trying to calm the nervous thumping of her heart. But a quick look in the mirror immediately grounded her anxiety, and her face crumpled with disgust and dismay at what she saw.

Her dark hair lay flat and lifeless against her head; the tip of her nose was a rosy, sunburned red, the same color as the oversized checked shirt that ballooned out from Max's baggy bibbed overalls. *I look like a rodeo clown,* she thought, blinking at the strange woman who blinked right back at her.

Lindsey scanned the length of her closet. What should she wear? Something . . . feminine, she thought. *Something that's mine,* she added silently, glancing down at the clothes she was wearing. Her teal silk blouse, maybe? She gazed at the slim black skirt in her closet. It was an old favorite, a reliable choice that on past dates had roused many compliments. And with her high-heeled black pumps—

Wait a minute! What was she thinking? *Max isn't here to be dressed up for,* she scolded herself silently. And it wasn't as if this were a date—not officially, anyway. They were just two people who went out fishing together, who were going to grab a bite of pizza—

She heard the knock at the front door. Pizza? Here, already? Lindsey listened to Max's muffled murmur, catching whiff of spice and tomato. Her stomach responded with a whine of anticipation.

Hurriedly, she stripped out of Max's clothes and stepped into a clean pair of jeans and a T-shirt. She wet her fingertips with her tongue and tried to spruce up her limp hair, but to no avail.

Oh, what the heck, she thought, opening the door.

She traipsed into the living room. "I have some pop in the fridge—"

Max was seated on her couch pouring red wine into two glasses. "I hope you don't mind. It was just sitting there on the cupboard."

Lenny's cheap table wine, his contribution to last night's spaghetti dinner.

"No—no, that's fine." She wiped her hands on her jeans, kicked her work boots into the corner behind the couch, picked up the empty potato chip bag on the coffee table, and collected the disarray of newspapers.

"Hey, don't clean up on my account." Max smiled. "Sit down. Relax." He patted the space next to him.

She sat down, passing a quick hand over her hair.

Max handed her a glass of wine. "Here's to all the fish we didn't catch, to good food . . . and good company."

They clinked glasses. Max sipped his wine, his hazel-brown eyes watching her over the rim as she raised the glass to her lips.

Lindsey smiled, hoping she didn't look as nervous as she felt. She selected a slice of pizza, then gazed at it, her eyes suddenly widening. "Wow," she murmured.

"You said 'anything.'"

"I didn't mean *everything*." She gave a low laugh and bit into the slice.

"Hmmm . . . not bad," murmured Max, chewing. He reached for his wine, gazing about her tiny living room. His eyes abruptly returned to rest on her and he set down his wine glass. He licked his lips, the corners of his eyes creasing. "Uh, you've got a little bit of sauce—" His finger touched his chin.

Lindsey ran her thumb along her chin.

"No, here. Let me." He leaned forward and dabbed at the spot beneath her lower lip. He hesitated, his face suddenly very close to hers.

Lindsey dropped her gaze, her heart pounding. She felt him pull away.

"I've been meaning to ask you about that . . . contraption." He pointed to the metal sculpture on top of the bookcase.

"Oh, that's—" Lindsey swallowed, following his gaze.

"That's a vesorium. It's designed to, er, detect electrical ... bodies." Her words tumbled out in a nervous rush. She noted, with some curiosity, the arrowed stick swinging back and forth, as if suddenly being pulled in several directions at once. *Strange,* she thought, *the stereo is on ...*

But the vesorium moved erratically, swinging from the stereo, to her bedroom, to the kitchen, and over to the couch where they were sitting—

"It doesn't seem to be able to make up its mind." Max raised his brows as the stick swiveled toward the stereo, then swung back in their direction. "There seem to be a lot of ... electrical bodies in this room," he murmured, gazing at her.

A sudden dizzying heat arrowed through her, and Lindsey reached for her wine. But Max's fingers moved to her hand, stopping her, and she looked up at him.

Like a charged magnet drawn to its mate, Lindsey found her body leaning toward him, inextricably drawn to this man sitting next to her. Max cupped her chin and she closed her eyes as his scent wrapped itself about her like a snare.

The shock of their meeting lips sent a jolt of pleasure ricocheting up her spine. The roots of her hair tingled.

"Magnetism is invisible..." The professor's words sifted through her as she felt Max's hand caress the back of her neck. His lips explored hers, gently at first, but as her arms came up to entwine about his shoulders, the kiss deepened. He pressed her close, his lips moving to trail along her cheeks and down along the contours of her chin. Lindsey could feel his chest heaving with hers, their hearts echoing fevered messages to one another.

He kissed her sunburnt nose, and buried his face in the hollow of her neck. "Oh, Lindsey," he rasped, "I've wanted to do this since the first time I saw you, sitting there on that bench at the fair."

Lindsey's voice fluttered in her throat. "Max, I—"

"Do you believe in love at first sight?" he murmured,

running his lips down her throat. But before she could answer, his mouth was on hers again, his scent closing in over her, claiming her.

Yes, she wanted to exclaim. *Yes, I believe in love at first sight.*

The harsh ring of the phone startled them, a thunderous sound that jarred them out of their embrace. Lindsey blinked at the phone on the coffee table. It rang again, and she answered it with a stunned and breathless: "H-hello?"

"Lindsey? Hi, it's Charlene. I hope I'm not disturbing you."

"Er—" Lindsey glanced at Max.

"Is Max there, by any chance?"

"Yes. Er, he's right here." She woodenly handed Max the phone.

Max frowned. "Hello? . . . Hi, Charlene . . . No, we were just—having some pizza." He cast a swift glance at Lindsey. "What? They're here? . . . I didn't expect them until Tuesday. . . . No, that's okay, I'll talk to them when I get home—Hey, Brian!" He straightened, shifting his body away from Lindsey.

" . . . Yes. . . ." He laughed. "No, we didn't catch anything. . . . Sure. I'll take you out this week. . . . Uh-huh. I heard about ol' Wily Wilbur." He nodded into the receiver. "Put your mother on the phone, will you? . . . Thea! When'd you get in?"

Lindsey got up and strode into the kitchen. But as she swept past the bookcase, she saw the vesorium pointer follow her, then swing back toward the stereo. She tried not to listen to the phone conversation, but with every new word Max uttered, her ribs tightened, slowly squeezing out her heartbeat. Her hands were cold weights as they distractedly rearranged items on the kitchen counter, waiting for the conversation to end—for Max to tell her he had to leave.

Max finally hung up. He sighed and stood up.

The Electric Cupid

Lindsey stood in the kitchen doorway, forcing a smile on her face. "Well, it was . . . fun," she said. But her words squeaked, her cheeriness ringing falsely even to her own ears.

"Yes, it was." Max glanced down at the phone, looking vaguely uncomfortable. "Lindsey, I—"

"It's okay." She shook her head and glanced at her watch; neither hand had moved; it was still five after one. "It's getting late, anyway."

"My sister and son have arrived from Saint Andrews," he explained. He looked down at the pizza. "I didn't expect them until Tuesday. But Charlene must have—"

"No need to explain," said Lindsey with a wave of her hand. "I understand."

Max hesitated.

"Go on. They're waiting for you." *Charlene's waiting for you. Is she staying at your house, as well?* she wondered.

"I'd like to see you—"

"Hey-ho! Lindsey girl!" Lenny opened the door. "Max! Well, hello there!"

Max picked up his jacket and greeted him with a smile. "Hi, Lenny."

"Hey, you're not leaving, are you? The night is still young. I just came up to ask Lindsey if—" He noticed then the pizza and the wine. "Whoa! I hope I'm not interrupting anything."

"Max was just on his way out," said Lindsey coolly. *Brrr . . . where did that coldness come from?*

"I guess you guys weren't as lucky as Miranda and me." Lenny thumped Max on the back. "That Miranda is some fisherman. And what a cook!" He patted his belly. "Well, I won't keep ya, Max. See you around, huh? Maybe all of us can go fishing sometime?"

"Sure," said Max, glancing back at Lindsey. "Can I . . . call you?"

"Anytime, Bud!" said Lenny, grinning.

Max waved and disappeared into the darkness.

Lenny closed the door. "Nice guy." His brows lifted. "So, you two had a good time, huh?"

"Uh-huh." Lindsey nodded, not really listening. Her head felt muzzy, and she swallowed back a sudden tickle in her throat.

". . . couldn't believe how much we have in common. She's just so—so . . . perfect. You know what I mean?"

Lindsey sighed; yes, she knew what he meant.

"At first, I was so nervous I was sweatin' buckets—hey! You listening to me?"

"What do you want, Lenny?" Her tone was terse.

"I just wanted to ask you if I could borrow one of your videos. All's I got are, well, martial arts and war stuff. I thought maybe . . . you know, something romantic—" Lenny's brows suddenly drew together as he gazed at Lindsey. "Hey, you okay? You look kinda . . . strange."

Lindsey touched her throat. "I think I might be coming down with something." She opened her cabinet, surveyed the rows of videotapes, and selected *The African Queen*. "Here. I think Miranda'll like this." She handed it to him.

"Yeah? Thanks." He turned it over in his hands. "Humphrey Bogart and Katharine Hepburn. Yeah, I think I've heard of 'em." He glanced over at her. "You sure you're okay, Lindsey? You don't look yourself."

"Probably just too much sun." She smiled, steering him to the door. "Better not keep Miranda waiting. She might get jealous."

Lenny swung open the door and laughed. "If anyone's going to be jealous, it's me. You and Max—well, gee, I can still feel the electricity in this room."

Lindsey sighed glumly. *Those are only the echoes of my heart.*

Chapter Ten

Lindsey awoke with a sneeze. She rubbed her eyes and swallowed, her hand moving to her throat. She sneezed again and the lump in her throat tightened like a vise. She sat up and swung her legs over the side of the bed. Her head throbbed with the movement.

"Oh no," she uttered nasally as she rose to her feet. Her head swam in dizzy response.

She shambled into the bathroom and stared at her reflection in dismay.

The two puffy, pea-sized eyes moved down to gaze at the swollen glands of her throat. Lindsey groaned. Great. First her wisdom tooth, now this. She sneezed.

She heard the phone ring in the living room. Lindsey's heart leaped up and turned over like a car ignition struggling to start a slow engine. She hesitated. Was it Max? On the fourth ring, she stepped out of the bathroom and strode into the living room.

Last night's pizza still lay, uneaten, on the coffee table. Lindsey gazed at the two wineglasses, one half-filled, the other drained empty.

The ring of the phone reverberated through her thoughts, making her wince. Lindsey sighed into the couch, massaging her temples. She sneezed twice, then reached for the phone.

She listened to the brief second of silence, then the dial tone.

Was that you, Max Rupert? Why are you calling me? To

apologize for last night? To tell me that kiss didn't mean anything? That it was all a mistake? That you've decided Charlene and you are right for each other, after all—that you're returning to Saint Andrews?

Lindsey cupped her face in her hands. She was feverish, that was all; she wasn't thinking straight. She picked up the phone and dialed Rhonda's number. After the third ring, she suddenly remembered her best friend was in Hawaii.

"Where are you when I actually need your advice?" she wailed.

She shuffled desperately through all of Rhonda's romantic platitudes, the words of wisdom Lindsey had shucked off over the years.

"Lindsey, you think too much." Rhonda would shake her head in bewilderment. "Why do you always try to sabotage every potential relationship before it ever begins?"

Yes, that's what she was doing, thought Lindsey, nodding to herself. She was thinking too much, and all these anxieties about Charlene, about Max leaving Boston, were just her way of sabataging their romance before it could even blossom.

Nonetheless, this revelation did nothing to alleviate her concerns. Her head pounded and her body ached with sudden weariness. She squinted at the stereo clock and was surprised to see that it was only seven-thirty. When had she finally traipsed off to bed last night? She'd watched the late-late mystery show, and stayed up to watch an exercise infomercial until the national anthem concluded station programming.

Sleep, that's what she needed. And then, maybe, she'd be able to think a little more rationally.

Lindsey dragged herself into the kitchen and opened her cupboards, searching for some cold remedies. She discovered an unopened bottle of vitamin C, and a crumpled package of Neo Citron shoved back behind some old cans of beans.

The Electric Cupid

As she heated water in the kettle, her thoughts drifted back to yesterday's adventures. Or rather, *misadventures,* she mused, remembering her inadvertent spill in the water, and their near arrest at Rhonda's house. She smiled. It was fun being out with Max, though—kissing him—

Perspiration suddenly sprang out on her forehead and upper lip. Her skin prickled hotly with the memory of Max's fingers caressing her neck, his hands pressing into the small of her back. If Charlene hadn't called—

Charlene. Cool, sophisticated Charlene. Lindsey conjured up that flawless porcelain skin, the graceful, poised way the woman slunk down the hall of Max's house. Was she there now? Lindsey could almost hear her conversing with Max's sister and nephew, trying to convince Max to leave Boston and come back with them to Saint Andrews.

The whistle of the kettle jarred her out of her dazed thoughts. She poured the hot water into the mug, watching the Neo Citron powder foam up to the surface. She opened the bottle of vitamin C and popped two tablets into her mouth.

Maybe this cold is a sign, she thought, shuffling out of the kitchen. *Maybe something is trying to warn me not to fall in love with this guy.*

But as Lindsey stood contemplating this new thought, she was suddenly conscious of a sudden movement to her left. She stared at the vesorium, watching its thin, finely balanced arrow swerve toward her like an accusing finger.

"Too late," it pronounced. *"You've already fallen in love, haven't you?"*

Lindsey pressed her hand to her chest as if to smother the persistent electrical echoes humming within.

And then she sneezed.

You can make it, Lindsey, she assured herself as she pulled on her jeans. She coughed, then sniffed, reached for another Kleenex and blew her nose. As she bent down to collect her work coveralls, her eyes suddenly fell on the red checked shirt. The bibbed fishing overalls were draped next to it across the chair.

"Oh, wonderful," she groaned aloud. Her head reeled and pounded as she straightened. Her body felt as though it had been pummeled from the inside.

It's all a state of mind; think healthy and you'll be just fine, she told herself. She pressed the palm of her hand to her burning forehead, willing the feverishness to go away. *Remember, you have the rewiring job at the Society of Arts and Crafts, and an ice cream machine to fix in Back Bay.*

Ice cream . . . mmmm . . . cool, creamy ice cream. She licked her dry lips and shambled into the kitchen to pour herself some orange juice.

She'd have to call Max about the clothes—or maybe she would just drop off the fishing overalls and shirt at his dental office. She glanced at her near empty glass and shook the empty orange juice container. And stop by the store to pick up some more orange juice. Some Tylenol, too. She wincing at the pain above her eyes. Maybe buy some chicken soup—and more Kleenex, she thought as she spied the empty box on the coffee table.

With a weary sigh she followed the trail of crumpled tissues strewn about the room. She shoved aside the splay of magazines and sank down on the couch. And while she was at it, she thought, shaking her head, she might as well hire a maid.

The digital clock on the stereo told her it was time to get cracking.

Twenty to seven. I'll just sit here for a few more minutes and make up the time on the freeway. Lindsey closed her eyes and her chin slowly nodded to her chest.

Cool, silvery water lapped around her as she floated on her back. The sky was a clear, cloudless blue empyrean

The Electric Cupid 139

above her, and she could hear the faint whisper of trees and birds chirping their cheerful tunes in the far distance.

"Gotcha!" The voice speared through the quiet, startling her. Lindsey's arms flailed as she lost her equilibrium and felt herself sinking down into the water. She tried to cry out, but no sound came.

She was aware, then, of a thrashing movement to her right. She turned, as if in slow motion, to see Charlene emerge from the depths like a beautiful porcelain figurine, her long black evening gown glistening and sparkling in the sun. As Lindsey continued to flounder in the water, Charlene flashed a triumphant smile at her.

"He caught *me,*" she said.

And all of a sudden Max's grinning face came into view. "She's got the right bait," he said with a shrug.

"But what about electricity?" But Lindsey's words were lost in the thunderous roar that crackled overhead.

Lindsey, losing strength now, felt herself being tugged down by the water's undercurrent. A spear of lightning lit the darkening sky as a damp warmth enveloped her, her body twirling, whirling out of control with the eddying motion of the river.

"Help!" she cried, reaching out her hand.

Fingers clasped her wrist and she stared up at Max's face.

"Bbrringg! Bbrringg!" he shouted, just as water closed over her face.

Lindsey jerked awake with a gasp.

She blinked, and stared down at the phone for a moment, suddenly lost to where she was.

The phone rang again, severing the lingering remnants of her dream.

"Heddo?" she answered.

"McGinty? Where in tarnation are you? You were supposed to clock in over an hour ago."

"Harry? I—" Lindsey caught a glimpse of the digital

clock: 8:44. "Oh, no! I must ob slebt in. Harry, I'm on my way—" She sneezed.

"Hey, McGinty, you don't sound so good."

"I'm fine. Just a liddle code, Harry. I'll be dere in—"

"You should've told me you were sick. Well, don't worry, Mike should be back in a half hour. I'll put him on the SOAC job—"

"I'm not dat sick, Harry." She coughed.

"Stay in bed. Drink plenty of fluids and, uh, yeah, vitamin C. Heat up some chicken soup while you're at it."

I don't have any chicken soup, thought Lindsey miserably. "Harry, I'm okay—"

"And get some rest, will ya?" Harry's tone was scolding. "I should've seen this coming. You've got sick days coming to you, anyway. Speaking of which, maybe you might want to think about that vacation—"

"I'm not taking a vacation," she cut in.

She heard him sigh into her ear. "Okay, okay. But you're not coming into work today, and that's final. Dr. Harry's orders. Rest up and get better, and I'll see you in a couple of days."

"Couble of days? I'll be in tomorrow." Lindsey stifled a sneeze.

"Whatever you say, McGinty." Harry exhaled loudly. And Lindsey could see him shaking his head, rolling his eyes, and rubbing that bald spot in weary defeat as he always did when confronted with her obstinacy.

Lindsey rang off and was surprised to find her irritation give way to an overwhelming sense of relief. It was true she had sick days coming to her—and when *was* the last time she took time off? Oh, yes. Now she remembered.

Her had went to her left cheek, and her tongue moved to the space where her wisdom tooth had once been. Max's grinning face loomed into her thoughts, and for a brief instant she conjured up the dream again.

Her T-shirt clung to her back, and she wiped absently at

the perspiration that streamed down from her hot forehead. She gave a little shiver as she rose to her feet. "Who turned up the air-conditioning?" she muttered angrily.

But when she checked the unit, she saw it was on its normal setting, and working fine.

I am *sick,* she thought. And with a surrendering sigh, she plodded back into her bedroom. Maybe "Dr. Harry's" advice wasn't so bad after all. Maybe she would take a vacation this year—

And go where? To Florida to visit her parents? No, she wasn't up to facing their all-too-familiar inquisition:

"Have you met anyone special, yet, Lindsey?... You know, dear, you're not getting any younger.... Whatever happened to what's his name? He was nice.... Lindsey, why don't you get married and settle down—give us some grandchildren?

... *We're* not getting any younger, you know.... Boston is full of good lads. Surely you can find one special 'someone,' someone who—how did you put it?—someone who sparks your interest?"

Yes, Mom, Dad—as a matter of fact I did meet that "special someone," she replied silently. She slipped into her pajamas and snuggled under her bedcovers, resting her head on the pillow with a weary sigh.

And yes, this special someone does spark my interest, she added, rolling over onto her side. She shut her eyes. She recalled how the vesorium had swung toward her and Max—for a moment, experiencing again the tiny electric shock she'd felt when they had touched.

Her thoughts drifted back then to her feverish dream, envisioning once again the triumphant look on Charlene's face as Max had hauled her out of the water.

Maybe, she sighed glumly, *electricity wasn't enough.*

Lindsey roused herself from sleep and lay on her back for a moment, staring up at the moonlit stripes on the far wall. She yawned and sniffled, swallowing back the dryness in her throat.

What time was it? She fumbled a hand toward her bedside table and turned the alarm clock face toward her.

Nine o'clock?! Oh no, I've slept the whole day away—

A noise stopped her. Lindsey sat up and listened. That sound had come from her kitchen.

The soft shuffle of feet. The sudden loud clatter of a pan being dropped, followed by a low curse. Lindsey's gaze slowly shifted. Electric light snaked in from the crack beneath her door. She hadn't left the lights on, she immediately thought. Come to think of it, she hadn't closed her bedroom door, either.

Someone was in her kitchen.

Lenny? He did have a key, yes. But why—?

Lindsey heard a low whistling, a cheery, upbeat tune she didn't recognize. No, definitely not Lenny; he couldn't carry a tune. She suddenly sniffed the air.

Someone was in her kitchen, cooking.

She threw back the covers and slid out of bed, holding back a sneeze. The hardwood floor was cold beneath her feet, and one of the floorboards creaked as she crept toward the door.

Careful, a voice in the back of her head warned. *It might be a burglar.*

Lindsey eased the door open, and squinted at the light. Curious . . . whoever was in her kitchen had managed to figure out how to switch on the standing lamp. Slowly, she poked out her head and craned her neck, peering round the door.

But from where she stood, she could make out only an elbow, a gray-trousered leg and the backs of her intruder's shoes. Shiny dress shoes.

She pushed open the door further and the hinges responded with a loud moan. The whistling suddenly stopped, and with her gaze still fixed upon those shoes,

Lindsey saw them shuffle, pause, and step toward the sound. She drew herself up and stared, transfixed, into the man's face.

"Well, hello there."

Lindsey gazed at him, caught off guard. "You! What—what are you doing in my kitchen?"

Max waved the wooden spoon in his hand like a magician's wand, and grinned. "I've come to nurse you back to health."

"How did you—?" She glanced in bewilderment at the front door, then at the standing lamp.

"Lenny let me in," said Max. "When you didn't answer the phone, I came over here to see if you were all right."

"I'm fine." Lindsey pursed her lips, struggling ineffectively to quash the tickle in her throat. She coughed, breaking her rigid stance.

Max's brow lifted. "Yes, I can see you're the picture of health." Amusement twinkled in his eyes as he swept a gaze over her disshevelled appearance. "You might want to put on a bathrobe. And you really shouldn't be walking around in your bare feet."

"I cad take care of myself—" She sniffed indignantly. "—dank you."

"Oh, I don't doubt that." Max grinned. "But I figured the least I could do was bring you over some cough medicine—since you don't seem to have any. And while I was at it, I thought I'd pick up some orange juice and some fruit." He smiled wryly. "Since you don't seem to have any of that either," he added.

Lindsey averted her gaze, wincing, suddenly aware of how she must look to him, standing there in her pajamas and bare feet. She didn't bother trying to comb her fingers through her mussed hair; she could feel each hair sticking up on its own like a petrified rooster.

"I'm not a child," she muttered. "I don't need looking after." But her eyes shifted to the pot of chicken soup.

Even with her nose feeling as though it were stuffed with cotton batting, the tantalizing aroma enticed her, making her stomach grumble, her mouth salivate.

"You didn't hab to go to all this trouble—"

"You can thank Mrs. Honeysuckle for the chicken soup," said Max. "She also recommends a nice hot bath and plenty of rest."

"Id smells good," said Lindsey with a small smile.

"Harry, on the other hand, recommends a vacation. He tells me you haven't taken one in over three years."

Harry. So that's how you found out I was sick.

"So, shall I run you a hot bath first? Or would you like to try some chicken soup?"

She let out a long sigh, which came out more like a congested moan. Feeling suddenly self-conscious and silly standing before him in her rumpled bedroom attire, she shook her head. "I-I dink I'll just go back to bed."

"Why don't you try some soup first?" he suggested. "Orange juice?"

I'd kill for some orange juice. She hesitated, licking her chapped lips. "Hmm . . . yes, maybe some orange juice," she relented with a croak and moved past him.

Max put his arm on her shoulder. "Uh-uh. I'll get it for you. You go put on some slippers."

Lindsey noticed then his tie, watching as he tightened the knot and adjusted the collar of his silk cotton shirt. His dark hair was coiffed back from his high forehead and he was clean-shaven. For a brief moment, their eyes met, and Lindsey quickly looked away, heat rushing to her face.

"I'm not an invalid." She frowned.

Max sighed. "You're not going to be an easy patient, are you?" He compressed his lips sternly. "If I have to, I'll carry you into the bedroom and dress you myself."

"Listen, you can't just barge in here and order me around—"

"Hmmm . . ." He consulted his watch. "I'm already late as it is. Charlene and the others are waiting for me at the Masquerade Theater."

"You have to go?"

Max looked at her, the corners of his lips turning up. His inquisitive expression abruptly turned to amusement, and he cocked an eyebrow. "And to think I had the feeling you didn't want me here."

"Well, no—I didn't mean—" She stammered, angry at the blush that crept into her cheeks.

"You can thank me later." He grinned. "When you're feeling better."

Lindsey nodded meekly.

Max scooped up his jacket from the couch. "Besides, I feel responsible for your, uh, condition."

Guilt? That's why you came over?

"Remember, chicken soup and a hot bath. The orange juice is in the fridge, and I put the cough medicine in the bathroom." He strode to the front door, opened it, then turned, gazing back at her. "And don't forget to put on your slippers."

Lindsey frowned, growling under her breath.

He waved and closed the door behind him. The standing lamp blinked out.

She sneezed, then coughed.

The door swung open again, and the standing lamp suddenly flickered as Max poked his head in.

"And while you're at it, you might want to think about taking a vacation."

As the door slammed shut behind him, the standing lamp switched off.

Lindsey stood for a long moment staring at it. How the heck did he get that lamp to work in the first place? She hadn't been able to turn it on for months now. She went over and reached for the switch beneath the lampshade.

But after a good twenty minutes of fiddling, she finally gave up.

Just beginner's luck, she thought with a shrug, and plodded off to her bedroom to find her slippers.

Chapter Eleven

Lindsey spent the next day cleaning up her apartment, purposely avoiding the phone and the standing lamp. Restless, she turned on the television, flicked the channels back and forth for an hour, then with a dissatisfied sigh, switched it off.

As she wandered about her apartment, she could feel the versorium's pointer dogging her movements. And the stubborn ever-presence of the standing lamp shadowed her like a tall, silent, guard, poised in ready challenge. She could feel it egging her on: *"All right, Miss Electrician, let's see you try to make me work. Turn me on, if you can."*

Instead, Lindsey pulled down her newly acquired *Echoes of Magnetism and Electricity* from the shelf, and nestled down in the couch. But barely had she finished the first paragraph when her mind began to meander.

Her fever had broke in the night, and Lindsey'd risen feeling better than she'd felt in a long time. Although her throat still ached and her nose twitched and tickled congestively, Lindsey felt more than ready to tackle the day's work.

"Why don't you take today off?" Harry had suggested. "You still sound a little groggy."

"I don't want to take the day off," replied Lindsey, sniffing.

"Well, I don't have anything for you, anyway. Just a bit of minor rewiring at a library."

"I'll do it."

"I've already given it to Sam."

"Sam? But he's just a first-year apprentice—"

"Come in tomorrow. We just landed a new contract with the Cambridge Castles apartment complex. A big installation job."

"Hey, great. Why don't I go down there—"

"No need. Mike and Alan are looking it over today. You just take it easy and get better, you hear?"

"But I'm feeling much better, Harry—"

"Glad to hear it, because I'm going to need you tomorrow, McGinty. Put your dogs up. Relax for a change. Think about how you're going to spend your upcoming vacation."

"I'm not taking a vacation this year, Harry."

But Harry ignored the air of finality in her tone, and merely harrumphed. "Just give me at least a few days' notice, okay? Mike's taking off to Mexico at the end of this month, and Christine's decided to leave me here with all this darn paperwork so she can go hand out with a bunch of bird peepers up in Canada somewhere."

"Don't worry, Harry. I'll be around to help you out."

"Not if you're out flat in a hospital bed, you won't."

"How many times do I have to tell you? I'm fine—"

"You need to learn how to relax. Nobody works three years straight without a vacation. I'm starting to get worried, McGinty."

"That's sweet of you, Harry, but—"

"There's nothing sweet about it. I'm just looking out for my best interest. This company's teetering on the edge of financial disaster as it is. All I need now is for one of my best employees to suffer a nervous breakdown—"

"Harry, I'm not having a nervous breakdown. I have a *cold,* that's all. And Elektron is not having any financial difficulties." She smiled then. "But thanks for worrying about me, boss."

"Yeah, well, someone has to—which reminds me. Max Rupert get a hold of you yesterday?"

Lindsey's heart gave a sudden involuntary lurch at the mention of Max's name. She thought about the chicken soup, and of what little remained in the fridge after last night's gorging.

"Er, yes. Max popped by." *More like sneaked in.*

"Nice fellow, Max." A sudden curiosity had crept into his tone. "Is there something between you two?"

"Max is just my . . . dentist," she answered tersely.

"Yeah, and Edith's my interior decorator," mumbled Harry. "Oh, speaking of which, Edith and I are having this barbecue thing this Saturday. Casual dress. We'll expect you at our place at six. Bring a date, if you like. Oh! Here's an idea. Why don't you bring your . . . dentist?"

And before Lindsey could retort, he rang off.

Why couldn't she admit she was attracted to Max Rupert? Certainly, she'd felt it—the spark of electricity that jolted her nerves, sending strange messages throughout her body whenever he was in a heartbeat's distance. And she could not deny that his kiss the other night had somehow electrified her—switched something on inside her.

Her eyes moved to the floor lamp next to the bookcase and she pulled her features into an expression of determined resolve. She stood, paused to blow her nose, and went to the closet to retrieve her toolbox.

A familiar *rat-at-tat-tat! tat-tat!* sounded at her door, and it promptly swung open.

"Hey-ho! Lindsey girl!"

Lindsey glanced up at Lenny from the floor where the standing lamp lay disemboweled, wires sticking up from its head like colorful, copper-tipped tentacles. "Hi, Lenny."

"Playing doctor?"

"Stupid thing won't work for me," she grumbled. But

it had worked for Max, she added silently; how had he managed to switch it on? Or rather, why couldn't *she* turn it on? And as far as she could tell all the necessary components appeared to be there. Somewhere there must be a glitch, a faulty wire—

"Feeling better, then, huh?" Lenny hunkered down beside her.

"Yeah." Lindsey nodded. "Max—" She glanced over at her downstairs neighbor. "Well, you let him in." There was a faint note of accusation in her tone.

Lenny shrugged. "Didn't think you'd mind. You were pretty out of it when we looked in on you. The chicken soup helped, then, did it?"

Lindsey began reassembling the floor lamp. "What do you want, Lenny?"

A look of mock hurt crossed his face and he rose, hitching up his jeans. "Gee, can't a guy just stop by to see how his favorite neighbor is doing?"

Lindsey quirked up an eyebrow.

"Okay, okay. You got me. I need a favor," he said, sighing. "It's Miranda. I just found out Thursday's her birthday, and I, well—I need your advice on a gift." He grimaced. "A nice gift," he added, smoothing back his wiry cowlick.

"Hmmm ... sounds like you're getting serious about this woman." Lindsey grinned, enjoying the flustered way his eyes darted about the room, taking in the uncharacteristic nervous flush that reddened his cheeks.

"Why don't you take her out to a dinner and a movie?"

"I am. But I—I'd like to buy her something. Something, you know—that women like." He paced around the living room. "I thought maybe you could come with me to the Faneuil Market and help me pick out something ... appropriate."

Lindsey glanced at her watch. She shrugged. "Sure. Just

give me a minute to clean her up." She gazed grimly at her patient lying prostrate on the floor.

She still wasn't sure the lamp would work, though the operation—as far as she could tell—appeared to have been an unnecessary one. As she tightened the last bolt, raised it back to standing position and capped on the shade, her fingers twitched in anticipation as they fumbled for the switch.

Nothing happened.

"Is it plugged in?"

Lindsey shot her neighbor a dour look. She plugged the lamp cord into the wall socket. The lamp remained stubbornly unlit.

Lenny shook his head and shoved his hands into his pockets. "Well, you can't save them all. Sometimes you've got to just let them go. Take my ol' girl, for instance. One minute she's roaring like a lion, and the next she's panting like an old mountain goat."

"So we're taking my truck, is that it?" Lindsey smirked, donning her jacket.

"Yeah." He grinned sheepishly. "The ol' girl has ... electrical problems."

So does this ol' girl, retorted Lindsey to herself.

Lenny pointed at a brooch inside the display glass. "How about that? It's kinda pretty, don't you think?"

Lindsey glanced at the price tag. "And kinda expensive. Who do you think you are? Rockefeller?" She threaded her way through the milling crowd, gazing at the display cases. "Maybe a pair of earrings—" Someone bumped into her from behind and her purse slipped off her shoulder.

"Oh! Excuse me—"

Lindsey glanced up at the woman as she bent down to retrieve her purse. Her look of surprise was mirrored in the woman's delicate porcelain features.

"Why, hello," said Charlene. A moment of chilled hesitation followed her greeting. "Fancy running into you ... here." Her smile held a plastic warmth as she cast a glance at the woman standing next to her.

"Er, yes." *Boston's not big enough for the two of us,* Lindsey retorted silently. She smiled at Charlene's companion, looked away for a second, then did a double take.

"Thea, this is Lindsey McGinty," introduced Charlene, her plastic smile hardening slightly. "Lindsey's one of Max's patients."

The woman extended her hand, her bright hazel-brown eyes gazing at Lindsey steadily. "Hello, Lindsey. I'm Max's sister."

As if I couldn't tell, replied Lindsey silently. Except for the arched brows, she was the spitting image of Max—right down to that cleft in the chin.

"Welcome to Boston, Thea. I hope you're enjoying—" She sneezed loudly.

"Oh, you're *that* Lindsey," said Thea, smiling sympathetically. "Max told us about your, uh, mishap on the weekend."

"Mishap?" And then her face reddened as she suddenly recalled her clumsy tumble into the river. So Max had told them about that. Lindsey pictured him and Charlene, sitting around the kitchen table with his sister and nephew, laughing as they listened to Max relate the tale of Lindsey McGinty's "mishap."

"I hope you're feeling better," said Thea. "I can't count how many times that's happened to me out on Passamaquoddy Bay. Once I even tipped over the boat." She laughed.

Lindsey's embarrassment faded, and she found herself laughing along with her. "Well, it was definitely an ... interesting experience. But I have to admit—I actually enjoyed it."

"Yes, Max is good company, isn't he?"

"Well . . . yes, I guess—" Lindsey could feel Charlene's catlike eyes shooting lasers through her.

Thea chuckled, shaking her head. Her shoulder-length hair, Lindsey noticed, was a lighter shade than Max's, but it curled up from that same high Rupert forehead. "Max is a born fisherman," she said, grinning Max's grin. "He practically lived out there on Passamaquoddy Bay."

"Yes, I think Max misses Saint Andrews," Charlene interjected. "This city's not exactly a haven for fishermen."

"But his practice here seems to be thriving," observed Thea. "And Boston is not quite what I expected." She shifted her gaze back to Lindsey. "You did some electrical work at my brother's house. I've never met a woman electrician."

Lindsey heard a throat clear behind her. She turned in time to see Lenny shuffle into step beside her.

"Hi," he greeted with a wave.

"Hello, Lenny." Charlene's smile narrowed her green catlike eyes.

"Lenny Bryce, this is Thea Rupert—"

"Mason," Thea corrected, shaking Lenny's hand.

"Thea is Max's sister. She's visiting from New Brunswick, Canada," said Lindsey.

Lenny hitched up his jeans and gazed at the woman, his eyebrows quirking together. "Max's sister? Yes, he said something about having family visiting him here in Boston. Are you the chef responsible for the chicken soup, then?"

"Chicken soup?" Thea frowned. Charlene looked equally confused.

"Er, Max brought me over some chicken soup yesterday—"

Thea's arched brows lifted. "Max made you his famous chicken soup?"

"He said Mrs. Honeysuckle, his dental assistant, made it," explained Lindsey, suddenly ill at ease.

"Oh, don't you believe it; Max is the cook in the Rupert

family," said Thea. "His chicken soup happens to be his specialty. But he's, uh, a little modest about his culinary abilities." She smiled at Lindsey. "As wonderful a chef as he is, he won't cook for just anyone. We usually have to beg him to cook for us."

Her curious, penetrating gaze made Lindsey flush. "I-I didn't know—"

"You should taste his veal parmigiana," interrupted Charlene. "Just last week he cooked up a beautiful romantic steak dinner for us."

Lindsey smiled uncomfortably, and a sudden awkward silence lapsed into the conversation.

"Well, it was nice bumping into you two," said Charlene with a strained porcelain smile.

"Yes. We'll tell Max we ran into you," said Thea. "He and Brian are out scouting fishing spots right now." She sighed. "My son certainly takes after his uncle, all right. On the plane over here all he could talk about was how many fish he and Max were going to catch. That—and that wild tale about Wily Wilbur."

Lindsey laughed. "'The Admiral of Passamoquoddy Bay.'"

Thea looked at her. "Oh, Max told you about that mythical old creature, did he? Well, I suppose these fishermen need their legends." She shook her head, rolling her hazel eyes. "Brian is still insisting that he caught this imaginary Wily Wilbur. And Max isn't exactly helping to dispel the myth."

"He was humoring Brian. Max knows there's no such fish," harrumphed Charlene.

Lindsey remembered Max's tale of how he'd managed to catch the old Admiral with the piece of cheese. Apparently, he wasn't lying when he'd confessed to Lindsey he'd not told anyone about it—not even Charlene. And for some reason, this sudden realization made her stomach flutter,

The Electric Cupid

stirring in the core of her being a new, warm, intimate feeling.

After they parted—with Charlene steering Thea briskly through the crowds—Lenny and Lindsey returned to the display cases.

"I don't think she likes you, Lindsey," he muttered.

"Who? Max's sister?"

"No." He shook his head. "Charlene. If looks could cook, you'd be roasting on a spit about right now—hey! How about those?" He pointed to a pair of enormous purple and gold hoops. "They're perfect for Miranda, don't you think?"

Lindsey drew back her lips, wrinkling her nose. Even Rhonda wouldn't be caught roasting on a spit with those.

The woman behind the case extracted the earrings from behind the display case and placed them in Lenny's palm.

He touched them gingerly with his finger and suddenly recoiled. He shook his hand in startlement. "Yow! I think I just got an electric shock!"

"Buy them," Lindsey said without thinking.

Chapter Twelve

Harry scanned the worksheets and glanced up over the stack of papers at Lindsey who was slumped in the chair, blowing her nose.

"So, your two days off give you any ideas, McGinty?" He leaned back in his chair steepling his hands together. "You look terrible, by the way."

"Thanks." She shot him a black stare.

"You know what you need? A vac—"

"Don't say it. I have a big enough headache as it is." But the fact of the matter was, all day Lindsey'd found herself seriously mulling over this idea of taking some time off. And yet, so long it had been since she'd gone on a real holiday, the concept seemed altogether alien to her. It was something that other people did—families, couples, newlyweds—not single women such as herself.

"Max Rupert called me."

Lindsey tried not to react. However, at the mention of his name, her heart performed a swift somersault, and she could feel a slow warmth worming its way up her body. "Oh?" she said, struggling to sound cavalier. She glanced down at her dirty nails. Charlene's beautifully polished talons immediately leapt to her mind. *I need a manicure,* thought Lindsey.

"He was looking for you," said Harry.

"Oh?" she said again, this time unable to quash the smile that played on her lips. The warmth metamorphosed

The Electric Cupid 157

into heat, and perspiration prickled beneath her arms. "He was looking for me?"

"His air conditioner is on the fritz," said Harry, studying his employee. "I sent Sam over to look at it."

Lindsey's stomach dropped.

"Hey, you sure you're feeling okay? You look a little ... out of it." Harry frowned at her in conncern. "You know, I can put Allan on the Cambridge Castles job—"

"No, no. I just—" She forced out a smile and rose to her feet. "I'm just a little tired, I guess."

Harry regarded her, thoughtfully rubbing the bald spot at the back of his head. "Well, not to sound like a broken record—"

Lindsey sighed. "I'll think about it, Harry." She started toward the door.

"See you Saturday?"

She waved back at him.

"And don't forget to ask Max!" he called after her.

Lindsey stood in front of Rhonda's hall mirror, her hands clasped together before her. She smiled at her reflection.

"Hello, Max. I would like to invite you to a barbecue on Saturday at Harry Lester's house—"

No, too formal.

She tilted her head slightly, resuming her smiling stance. "Hello, Max. I was wondering, if you're not busy Saturday evening ... you see, there's this barbecue Harry and Edith are having, and so, er, I was wondering ..."

What are you? Sixteen?

"Hi, Max. You busy Saturday evening? ... No? Great. You interested in going to a barbecue with me?"

What if he says no?

She unclasped her hands and rested them firmly on her hips, narrowing her dark brown eyes slightly.

"Max. Hi. You and me—Saturday. Six o'clock. Barbecue at Harry's place—"

Right. Lindsey sighed. *I'm going to bully him into going.*

She folded her arms across her chest, assuming a calm, controlled pose.

"Hello, Max. If you like, you can come to a barbecue with me on Saturday—"

The phone interrupted her.

Lindsey strode into the kitchen to answer it.

"Lindsey!" Rhonda's voice squealed into the receiver. "How goes it in dull ol' Boston?"

"It's the same as you left it, Rhonda." Lindsey grinned. "You sound drunk. I hope you left some of that Hawaiian Punch for the rest of the natives."

"Oh, you wouldn't believe how beautiful it is here! Even Rick's become smitten with this place. You should see him, Lin. I can't tear him away from the beach. He's like this twenty-four-hour lawn chair. You won't recognize him when we get back. Well, you won't recognize *me*. I'm like a shiny new penny! The weather's been great! Oh, Lindsey, you've got to come out here!"

"You know me. I'm liable to turn into a lobster—or get sunstroke."

"Same old Lindsey." She chuckled. "But you sound a little funny. Are you okay?"

"I'm just getting over a little cold," said Lindsey, sniffling.

"You're working too hard. What you need is a vac—"

"Don't say it!" Lindsey sighed. "Harry's been on my back about taking time off."

"Well, he's right, you know. Oh—Rick's signaling me. How're my plants doing?"

Lindsey gazed at the massive philodendron whose leaves bordered the length of the kitchen cupboards. She eyed the ivy on top of the cabinet, the blooming African violets clustered around the kitchen table. A row of pepperomias and jade plants peeked out at her from the dining room. With the myriad of plants sprawled about the living room and upstairs, it had taken Lindsey close to an hour to finish watering them all. *Hmm... with Max, it'd taken them twenty minutes.*

"Don't worry, Rhonda. Your plants are doing better than I am."

A beat passed.

"Is that your cold talking—or has something else happened?"

And before Lindsey could respond, Rhonda went on: "So how's the dentist?"

"The dentist?"

Rhonda breathed a heavy sigh in her ear. "Don't play innocent with me, Lindsey. You know who I'm talking about. Your dentist... Max Rupert?"

"Oh, well—"

"So did you end up going on that date of yours?"

"It wasn't a date. We went... fishing, that's all."

"All right! So you went, after all."

"How do you think I got this cold?"

"And—?" prompted Rhonda.

"And nothing. It-it was... fun."

"Are you going to see him again? Oh—I have to get off the phone. Rick's giving me the evil eye." Lindsey heard Rhonda mutter something to her husband. "Lin? I'll see you Sunday, then, okay? Now, don't do anything I wouldn't do—no, ex that. *Do* what I would do. And Lindsey, if you like this Max guy, don't let him get away. Ask *him* out. Guys love that—okay, okay!" she exclaimed to her husband. "Well, gotta go. The beach beckons. Aloha! as they say in Hawaii."

Lindsey hung up and stood for a moment, thinking.

"Hey, Max! Wanna go to a barbecue with me on Saturday?"

She winced and shook her head; what was wrong with her? It was just a stupid barbecue—not a marriage proposal. Why was she so nervous? What could be the worse that could happen?

He could say "yes," a voice in the back of her mind answered.

With grim resolve, Lindsey mustered together her thoughts, and took a deep breath. She reached for the phone. But as her hand hovered over the receiver, it all of a sudden dawned on her that she didn't have his number. And then she remembered the business card she'd tossed on the dashboard of her truck. She started for the door.

The phone stopped her.

She answered it, exhaling her breath at the same time. "Hello?"

"Hi, Lindsey. It's Max."

"Oh." Lindsey pressed the heel of her hand to her chest, suppressing the rise of an echoing beat behind her ribcage. "Hi," she said breathlessly.

"I didn't catch you at a bad time, did I?"

An echo resonated beneath her palm. "Er, no. I was just—" *Going to call you,* she almost replied. She swallowed back the tickle in her throat. "I was just on my way out."

"You're a hard woman to track down. Thea says she ran into you yesterday."

"Yes." *Ask him!* "Er, Max? I was wond—"

"I'm glad you're feeling better. The chicken soup helped, I see."

Your chicken soup, she amended silently. "Yes." She let a beat pass. "Listen, Max—"

"The reason I'm calling—well, you see, I've promised to take Brian fishing on Saturday," he explained. "I meant to pick up my pants the other night, but, I, uh, guess I got sidetracked."

"Oh." Lindsey bit her lip.

"So, I was wondering if I could come over and pick them up. Say, tomorrow evening?" Lindsey heard a woman's voice in the background—Charlene's voice. "Oh, right," he said to Charlene, then to Lindsey: "Or perhaps, Friday afternoon?"

Friday she would be working all day at the Cambridge Castles complex. "I'll be at work," she said.

Muffled static hissed in Lindsey's ears. ". . . You sure?" he said, continuing an ongoing conversation. "Lindsey? Are you going to be home later tonight?"

Another echo pulsed through her. "Yes, I'll be home."

"Great. Charlene said she'll drop by your place on her way home and pick up my things."

The echo fizzled. "Oh. Sure—okay."

"Thanks, Lindsey."

Just before she hung up, her ears caught the tail end of a voice that squeaked loudly in the background: ". . . are you coming back with us to Saint Andrews, Uncle Max?"

Lindsey frowned at the telephone. Something turned over in her stomach and tightened like a fist. An ache throbbed behind her eyes. And as she made her way to the front entrance, she glimpsed her expression in the hall mirror. Her features were bunched up and the corners of her eyes tugged downward. She stuck her tongue out at her reflection and swung open the door.

As she locked the door behind her she waved at Mrs. Olafson, who immediately withdrew behind the safety of her curtains. Lindsey climbed into her truck and sank into the seat with a heavy sigh.

Her eyes immediately fell upon the business card on the dashboard. She reached over and picked it up, thumbing it as she read the scrawled phone number on the bottom. For a brief instant Lindsey's fingers curled around it, preparing to tear it up. But the moment passed, and instead, she found herself tossing it back on the dashboard.

Well, he hasn't left for Saint Andrews yet, she thought, driving off with a determined grimace.

* * *

It was almost eleven o'clock when Charlene finally showed up at her door.

"Hello, Lindsey. I've come for Max's things," she greeted with a tepid smile. A porcelain hand reached up to pat her strawberry blond hair which was swept up into a neat, delicate bun. Her swan-pale throat gleamed like polished ivory.

The bibbed fishing overalls and the checked shirt were neatly folded on the couch, and Lindsey wordlessly handed them to Charlene.

"Interesting place you have, Lindsey," commented Charlene, her gaze sweeping across the living room. Her pinched expression chilled her words, and her catlike eyes narrowed as they came to rest on Lindsey. "I've never been into garage sales, myself—but a person's living environment does tend to reflect one's personality—and taste."

Have I just been insulted? Lindsey moistened her lips, the force of her smile making her face ache. "I suppose I am a little sentimental," she admitted, glancing over at her old faded couch, a MIT graduation present from her parents.

"Yes. You're just like Max, that way," said Charlene, caressing the bibbed fishing overalls. "He's sentimental—not so much about . . . things, though. Since Thea and Brian have been here, all he's been talking about is Saint Andrews this, Saint Andrews that. He's obviously been missing his weekend fishing trips at Passamaquoddy Bay. The fishing here in Boston doesn't even compare with Saint Andrews, he says."

Lindsey nodded, attempting to wade through the tension that seeped from this woman and thickened a chokehold around her apartment. She wished this woman would just take Max's things and go.

But Charlene went on, her smile wary. "Ah, but it was

The Electric Cupid 163

inevitable," she said, smugness now tugging at her delicate pink lips. Her sigh held a note of triumph.

"Yes, it was inevitable that Max would soon tire of this city. After all, Boston isn't Saint Andrews," she added, and the look she cast Lindsey was that of a cat who has just succeeded in pinning her defenseless prey.

"Well, it was nice meeting you, Lindsey." She turned on her heel, opened the door, and strolled out, the silky fabric of her dress swaying with her slender hips.

Lindsey closed the door and leaned against it as if fearing Charlene's cloud of doom might force itself back into her apartment. Her relief, however, was but a transient thing, for now what hung in the air was worse.

Max was leaving Boston.

Her gaze lifted, searching out her bookcase, pausing for a moment to rest on the vesorium. The thin, arrowed pointer seemed almost to sag in its energyless path. To its right the floor lamp stared back at her from beneath its dark shade.

Someone has switched off all the electricity, thought Lindsey miserably.

The days leading up into the weekend passed with numbing listlessness for Lindsey. Even Rhonda's imminent return from Hawaii did not spark in her any enthusiasm.

Friday, after she finished her work in the main electrical unit at the Cambridge Castles apartment complex, she begged off an invitation to celebrate Mike's upcoming vacation farewell, and retired to her own apartment in brooding silence.

That night, Lenny found her sprawled on her couch watching television. He'd popped by to let her know how much Miranda had loved her birthday gift.

"I'm tellin' ya, Lindsey, I've never felt this way about a woman before," he gushed. "It's like—like she turns on all these switches in me. I swear I can feel myself lighting up like a darn fool Christmas tree when she's around.''

"That's nice," said Lindsey dully.

He perched himself on the arm of the couch. "It's great, isn't it? Having that instant connection with someone." He leaped up, gesturing with his hands. "Zap! Well, you know what I mean—like with you and Max."

Uh-huh. Like me and Max, thought Lindsey, fixing her neighbor with a weary, ironic gaze.

"It's—it's like you've just been zapped with ten thousand volts of electricity," he went on dreamily.

It's not the volts, but the amps that'll do that to you, corrected Lindsey silently. "Hmmm . . . you may be right about that, Lenny. Love'll definitely fry your brain." She reached for the remote control and flicked the channel.

Bridges of Madison County was playing, and Meryl Streep and Clint Eastwood were dancing together in the kitchen. Lindsey quickly pressed the channel-change button. The camera zoomed in on a bride and groom exchanging vows in a Las Vegas church. As the camera angle widened, viewers could see a paunch-bellied Elvis look-alike, complete with sunglasses and white sequined jumpsuit, undulating and bobbing his head as he sang a classic Elvis Presley song.

Lindsey simulated a gagging response and flicked the channel. Dax and Warf from "Deep Space Nine" were engaged in a Klingon mating duel. Flick.

Ah, good ol' sock-'em, chop-'em "Xena, Warrior Princess"—Lindsey's eyebrows suddenly quirked up, her eyes squinting at the screen. Who was that man Xena was kissing?

Lindsey groaned aloud and shut off the television.

"Hey! I was just starting to get interested in that," complained Lenny.

"You watch Xena?"

A dizzy look came into his eyes, and he hitched up his

jeans, smoothing his wiry cowlick away from his forehead. "Miranda likes Xena."

Lindsey rolled her eyes, picked up an issue of *Electric Entertainment* from the coffee table, and began flipping through it, bored. "Let me know when you get back from Planet Love, will you?"

Lenny furrowed his brow, eyeing his neighbor quizzically. "Say, Lindsey, you don't look so hot. That cold still bugging you?"

Lindsey shook her head. "Nope. I'm 100 percent over it." She let out a small cough and grimaced. "Okay, 95 percent." Then, why did she feel 100 percent terrible? she wondered miserably.

"You have any plans tonight?"

Lindsey looked at him. "Does it look like I do?" Her tone, she remarked, was a tad too quick, her irritation showing plainly in her expression.

"Well, I thought, maybe you and Max—"

"Max and I—" She pursed her lips. "Max is my dentist." She flipped through the magazine. "Although it looks like that will be changing soon enough."

"What do you mean? Is Max leaving dentistry, or something?" asked Lenny, scratching the back of his neck.

"Not dentistry," said Lindsey, her eyes fuzzing over as she tried to concentrate on the magazine article.

"Am I missing something?" queried Lenny. "Something happen between you two?"

Yes—electricity, thought Lindsey. Her lips blazed beneath the tips of her fingers as she retraced the memory of Max's kiss. It was right here, on this very couch—

"Lindsey?" Lenny snapped his fingers in her face. He inclined his head, observing his neighbor. "Now, who's off on 'Planet Love,' eh?" He laughed, and dismissed her gesture of protest with a wave. "Hey, give me some credit. I'm not a cement head; I may be dense, but I'm not *that* dense. I've seen the way you and Max look at each other."

"Lenny—" Lindsey began with a groan.

"I mean, you should've seen him when he came to see me that night." Lenny smiled knowingly. "And the way he looked at you." He glanced over in the direction of her bedroom. "You were snoring so loud I thought the roof would cave in."

"I don't snore."

"Uh-huh." He chortled. "Oh, by the way—I gave him your spare key."

Lindsey sat up. "You what?!"

He shrugged and hitched up his jeans. "Well, I figured it was okay, seeing that you and he—"

"There is nothing going on between Max and me," said Lindsey. But her protest stuck in her throat, and her voice faltered a little. She sighed and lay back on the couch, staring up at the ceiling. If only this miserable feeling in her gut would go away.

Lenny, deaf to her words, passed his hand nervously over his wiry hair and sucked in his stomach. "Well, when you see him, thank him for the advice, will ya?"

"Advice? Advice on what?"

Lenny wiggled his brows. "That's secret. You know, guy stuff."

Lindsey snorted.

"Well, I'm off. How do I look?" He preened a macho pose.

Lindsey glanced at him, then frowned slightly. Now that she looked at him, she sensed something a little different about him. But he was wearing that same white shirt, that same old black leather vest, and those jeans that didn't quite fit. She glanced down at his cowboy boots. "Hmmm ... you look—nice, Lenny."

He smiled, winked, and whistled between his teeth. "See ya later, Lindsey girl."

The Electric Cupid

Lindsey watched Lenny stroll out the door. She shook her head in bemusement. For a moment there, she'd almost thought her downstairs neighbor had actually grown taller.

She flicked the television back on, turned to the shopping channel and relaxed into boredom, trying to wipe clean her mind of Max Rupert . . . and electricity.

Chapter Thirteen

"So, let me get this straight." Rhonda sipped her coffee. "He comes here to Boston, opens a dental practice, buys a house—and now he's going to go back to—?"

"Saint Andrews." Lindsey bit into her cruller.

Skepticism rippled across Rhonda's newly bronzed face. "That's crazy. It doesn't make sense."

Lindsey shrugged. It was beginning to make perfect sense to her now; Max missed his hometown, the place where he'd grown up—where all his family and friends still lived. It was in Saint Andrews, after all, where he'd first learned how to fish, where he'd first fallen in love—with Charlene.

"And he told you this? That he was leaving Boston?"

Lindsey stirred her coffee. "Yes—well, no. Actually, it was Charlene who told me."

"Charlene? You mean his receptionist?"

"His high school sweetheart," corrected Lindsey.

"But they're—" Rhonda scratched her head. "Charlene and Max—they're not involved, not *romantically*, are they?"

"From what she told me—"

"But Max didn't tell you this, did he?"

Lindsey sipped her coffee glumly. "He didn't have to."

Rhonda vented an impatient sigh, rolling her eyes. "And you actually believed her?"

"Why wouldn't I?"

The Electric Cupid 169

"Lindsey, are you blind? Don't you see what that woman's trying to do?"

"Rhonda, let it alone."

Rhonda regarded her friend, her exasperation giving way to sudden real concern. "You're really stuck on this guy, aren't you?"

Lindsey avoided her gaze. "Naw." she shrugged and forced her lips into a weak smile. "And anyway, there are plenty of fish in the sea, right?"

But Rhonda, who knew her friend, looked unconvinced. "Why don't you call him, Lindsey. Straighten this all out."

Lindsey shook her head. "There's nothing to straighten out." But he still had her house key; if she did ring him up—"No, that's not my style," she said aloud, as if to herself.

"*This* isn't your style." Rhonda gesticulated with open palms. "You moping like this—giving up. Lindsey, it's not like you to bow out of a competition. If you want to catch this guy—"

"Rhonda, this isn't some kind of... fishing expedition." Lindsey rubbed her temples in weary frustration. "I mean, he has to want to be caught, right?"

"And? Your point being?"

Lindsey moaned. "I don't know. Okay—maybe, maybe, I thought when he kissed me—"

Rhonda's brows shot up. "He kissed you? Wait a sec. You never told me about that!"

Lindsey flushed. "Well, it wasn't really anything..." She rolled her lips between her teeth as if to hide their telltale heat. But the hairs at the nape of her neck stood at attention, and her heart gave an involuntary tug at the memory of his warm hands, the kisses that still burned a trail along her throat. She coughed.

"You've got to call him, Lin."

* * *

Lindsey picked up the phone, glanced at the number scrawled on the business card, listened for a moment to the dial tone, then hung up. She did this four times before she slumped back against the couch in defeat.

What's wrong with you, Lindsey? Where's that old competitive spirit? You've never been one to back down from a fight.

Fight? What fight? She glanced down at her palms. They were sweating. "What the heck am I doing?"

Just call him and get it over with, nagged the voice in the back of her mind.

Lindsey compressed her lips and reached for the phone. It rang just as her fingers closed over the receiver.

"McGinty?"

"Harry?"

"So where the heck were you yesterday?"

The barbecue. "Oh, Harry, I'm sorry. I forgot all about the barbecue."

"Well, you missed a humdinger," said Harry. "Oh, by the way, Max Rupert showed up. He tried to call you, but your line was busy."

Lindsey grimaced; she'd purposely taken the phone off the hook, hoping that an uninterrupted evening alone might improve her gloomy mood. It hadn't helped, of course. "Er, yes, this phone's been giving me some trouble," she lied. So, Max showed up at the barbecue?

"Yeah, well, Edith invited . . . your dentist a few days ago. He was real disappointed you didn't show up. Said he had something real important to tell you. And you missed a great wing-ding." He laughed. "Allan and Tim rented some karaoke equipment. . . ."

Max had something important to tell me? Had he decided, then, to go back to Saint Andrews? Perhaps he wanted to return her key, apologize for the kiss, for making her think—

The Electric Cupid   171

Think what? That his kiss meant something? That she'd only imagined the electricity she'd felt between them?

Lindsey's head ached with her inconclusive questions, "maybes" and "perhaps" dizzying around like a merry-go-round in her thoughts. She shut her eyes tight, trying to make sense of the jumble inside her mind.

Call him, a voice cut in abruptly.

"... and, you know, I have to say, Max has the worst singing voice I've ever heard—present company excluded, of course." Harry laughed.

"Yes, I've heard you sing, Harry."

"You okay, McGinty? You sound kind of . . . groggy."

"Must be the connection. I'm having trouble with this phone—"

"So you said." Harry didn't sound convinced. "Well, we missed you at the barbecue. You're the only one with a decent singing voice—although young Sam might actually give your voice some competition."

"Oh?" Lindsey's back straightened. "He's better than me?"

There was a short pause. "Nah. You're still number one, as far as I'm concerned." He sighed. "You're also my most stubborn employee."

"Persistent, you mean."

Harry snorted. "Competition is in your blood, McGinty. I pity anyone who challenges you. They don't know what they're getting into." Lindsey pictured him rubbing that bald spot on his head. "Right now, you're holding out for the employee record for longest consecutive work hours without a vacation."

"Oh? Who has the record now?"

A beat passed.

"You do, McGinty."

She listened to the phone ring in her ear, her heart pounding in her throat, her fingers drumming nervously.

"Hello?" purred a woman's voice—Charlene's voice.

"Hello, may—" Lindsey cleared her throat. "May I speak to Max, please?"

"Who is this, please?" A note of wariness singed the line.

"Er, Lindsey. Lindsey McGinty."

"Oh. Max is just loading the luggage in the car. I'm afraid we're just on our way out, Lindsey. Oh—he's honking. I'm sorry, but we're in a bit of a rush. I'll tell him, though, that you called to say good-bye." And she hung up.

Lindsey blinked at the phone. "Good-bye"? She hung up, stunned. Was Charlene telling the truth? Was Max really leaving Boston? After a moment, she dialed the number again, but after the eleventh ring she hung up.

Her rib cage closed in on her chest, and an overwhelming sense of being crushed from the inside out made her breath hiss out of her in short gasps. She needed to get out—get some fresh air. She leaped to her feet, grabbed her purse and dashed out of the apartment. As she climbed into her truck she thought she heard her phone ring. She paused, listening. Yes, it was her phone.

Max. It was Max; she was sure of it. She raced back up the front walk and fumbled with the key, cursing herself for not fixing the lock.

"I'm coming!" she yelled at the phone inside. She flung open the door and propelled herself toward the phone on the coffee table.

"Hello!" she answered breathlessly.

A click.

"Hello! Hello!"

The drone of the dial tone echoed hollowly in her ear. "Darn!" She hung up with a grimace. Was it Max? she wondered and dialed *69. The computerized voice read out the number.

Lindsey's heart soared. Yes! It was him! He hadn't left yet.

She quickly dialed Max's number.

"Woo Yung Chinese Cuisine. How may I help you?" a heavily accented voice answered.

Lindsey slammed down the phone, glanced at the business card on the table, and redialed.

It rang, and rang.

"Come on, pick up," she murmured impatiently.

The phone continued to ring. Lindsey sank down on the couch, the receiver still to her ear. Her apartment appeared to darken all of a sudden. The summer twilight colors cloaked the room in graying shadows, the floor lamp maintaining its silent, brooding vigil. Over the bookcase, the vesorium's arrow was suddenly still, pointing at nothing.

She'd missed him.

With a surrendering sigh, Lindsey finally hung up, and admitted defeat.

Lindsey glanced back again at the figure perusing the racks of sports jerseys. Her heart bleated a beat as she paused in her step. For a split second, she'd thought it was Max. But as the tall figure vanished into the store, the bleating in her chest slowed and her stomach muscles grew lax.

She'd glimpsed the rounded, curvy physique, the leather purse swinging from the person's shoulder; the figure was a woman.

"Lindsey? You listening to me?" Rhonda nudged her.

"Oh, sorry. I thought . . . I saw someone I knew." *How could I've mistaken that woman for Max?*

But still, there had been something altogether too familiar about that woman—the dark hair swept up from the high forehead, the way she'd inclined her head, the slow movement of her shoulders—

Rhonda gave her friend a slow, understanding smile. "You thought you saw Max, didn't you?" She glanced down at her watch, and grimaced. "Oh! I didn't realize how late it was. We should start heading back. A couple of Rick's clients are coming over for drinks this afternoon."

"I'll drop you off," nodded Lindsey absently.

Rhonda grinned, a mischievous glint brightening her eyes. "Or you could stop in. Ernie Watson's going to be there."

"No thanks, Rhonda. I-I'm not really up to meeting any new people just right now."

"It's him, isn't it?" Rhonda opened the door, and they were met with a rush of heat. "Whew! This heat is unbearable! It was never like this in Hawaii." She looked over at her friend. "You know, Lindsey, you really should consider taking a vaca—"

"I'm still thinking about it, Rhonda."

"Among other things." Rhonda quirked up an eyebrow. "One person in particular, I might name," she mumbled.

They climbed into the truck, their clothes clinging to their bodies, their bodies glistening with sweat. Lindsey reached over to turn on the air-conditioning.

The truck sputtered, spewing out a noise much like that of a plane engine giving up in mid-flight. "Not now! Air-conditioning, don't quit on me now!" But the air that streamed through the vents was anything but cool.

Rhonda dabbed her forehead with the sleeve of her T-shirt. "Electrical problems?"

"Hmmm . . . I seem to be having a lot of those kinds of problems these days," grumbled Lindsey.

"They have phones in Saint Andrews, you know," said Rhonda. "And don't they have an airport nearby? Why don't—"

Lindsey shut her friend up with a warning stare.

"You want to come in and cool off for a bit?" Rhonda invited.

Lindsey billowed her sweaty T-shirt up and down like a fan, and wiped her prespiring face. "I think I just might," she nodded.

Rhonda put her hand on Lindsey's arm. "It'll take some time, but you'll get over him, Lin."

Lindsey shrugged. "What's to get over? Max is gone, right? What am I going to do? Chase him all the way to Saint Andrews?"

"Hmmm . . . well, you are thinking about a vacation—"

"Rhonda!" Lindsey rolled her eyes. But it wasn't as if that thought hadn't crossed her mind. Oh, she could see herself now: knocking on his door, and Charlene answering—

"Hello, girls," greeted Mrs. Olafson from her driveway as they came up the front walk. The taxi reversed and sped off.

"Hello, Mrs. Olafson. Hot enough for you?" greeted Rhonda.

"I've been at the dentist all day," said Mrs. Olafson, gingerly touching her cheek. Her eyes immediately moved from Rhonda to Lindsey. After a moment, recognition lit her face and she addressed Lindsey.

"You tell your boyfriend I think he's a real fine dentist. I never liked going to the dentist until I met Dr. Rupert. And I like that Mrs. Honeysuckle. But that receptionist of his—well, all I can say is, I won't be shedding any tears when she leaves." She fingered her jaw and grimaced a little, but her cheerful demeanor remained. "I was just telling Dr. Rupert that in my day—"

Lindsey stared at the older woman. "You've just been to see Max—I mean, Dr. Rupert?"

"Yes. I just returned from there." Mrs. Olafson nodded.

"Today? You mean, today?" said Rhonda, exchanging a look with Lindsey.

Mrs. Olafson pressed her hand to her cheek. "Yes, of

course today!" She harrumphed, strolling past her cedar hedges and up the front steps. Evidently, from her glowering expression, she thought Lindsey and Rhonda were making fun of her.

"You're talking about *Max* Rupert, right?" Lindsey called over.

The Watchful Widow paused before her open door and glanced over at Lindsey, the heat beginning to flush her normally sallow cheeks. She shook her head and seemed about to say something, but only pursed her lips and entered her house.

"He hasn't left yet," said Rhonda, squeezing Lindsey's arm. "Now's your opportunity, Lin! You've got to go see him!"

"But I don't understand—" It didn't make sense to her. "Why'd he come back?" she thought aloud.

"Maybe he never left?" ventured Rhonda.

If he hadn't left, then why hadn't he called her? But for the past week, Lindsey'd been working double shifts, spending the majority of her evenings at the Gatland Factory rewiring assembly lines. And she'd taken the phone off the hook on Thursday, not remembering to replace it until this morning when she'd come to pick up Rhonda.

It just might be that all this time Max had been trying to contact her—

Lindsey's drumming heartbeat drowned out her thoughts, and her hand moved to quiet the queasy excitement that was suddenly roiling in her stomach.

"Go! Go see him!" Rhonda pushed her back down the front walk. "And try not to think on your way there. I know you; you'll talk yourself right out of seeing him. Lindsey, this might be your last opportunity. Grab it while you can!"

Lindsey glanced down at her sweaty clothes, and passed a hand through her short damp hair. She looked a mess. "Maybe I'll call him—"

The Electric Cupid

Rhonda had already guided her to her truck. "Okay. Call him. But remember, don't think. Just do it."

Okay, so I call him, tell him how I feel—And then what? thought Lindsey as she climbed into her Toyota and waved at Rhonda.

Don't think, she reminded herself. *Just go home and call him. Whatever happens, happens.*

However, as she turned off Watertown Street and veered down Globe, her heart began to pound with the roar of the truck's engine. She tried to moisten her lips, but her tongue seemed to suddenly thicken inside her dry mouth. Doubt flooded her mind, and new thoughts swelled in her head.

If Max was leaving Boston, what good would it do her to tell him she was crazy about him? She was a fool to think she could compete with Saint Andrews, not with his family pressuring him to return, with Passamaquoddy Bay and ol' Wily Wilbur enticing him back, and . . . Charlene.

She sidled up into the driveway behind Lenny's rusty camero. She glimpsed a blue Taurus parked on the shoulder. Miranda's car, she guessed. Wait a minute—didn't Charlene drive a Taurus?

Lindsey immediately dismissed this thought. What would Charlene be doing here? Charlene: the woman who had made it clear the last time they spoke that she and Max shared a history together—a history that still bound them to the present, to the future.

And where did she fit into all this? mused Lindsey, turning the key in the front door. Nowhere, she answered glumly; she was a Bostonian, an outsider. Okay, so she could not deny these feelings Max had aroused in her, with his mere presence somehow managing to electrify her entire being. Still, this didn't mean he felt the same electricity—

The floor lamp greeted her blinking eyes with a steady brilliant stare, its yellow light illuminating the room like a search beacon.

"What the—?"

"It just turned itself on," said a voice.

Lindsey jumped. "Yaah!"

The owner of the voice rose from the couch and grinned. "Sorry. Didn't mean to startle you."

Lindsey tried to quieten the brass band in her chest. "You nearly gave me a heart attack! What are you doing here? How did you—"

Max held up the key. "I forgot to return this." His hazel-brown eyes lingered over her sweat-stained T-shirt and shorts before he turned his attention back to the floor lamp. "That's some motion detector you've got there."

Lindsey shot the lamp an exasperated look. "It—it just came on?"

He nodded. "It did the same thing when I came in that night to, uh—when you weren't feeling well." He smiled, shoving his hands in his pockets. "I see you're feeling much better."

"Thanks to your chicken soup."

"Well, Mrs. Honeysuckle—"

"Your sister, Thea, told me chicken soup is one of your specialities," said Lindsey, shutting the door.

Max frowned, his composure wavering slightly. "Hmmm . . . I've been found out. Well, my culinary habits aren't usually something I talk about."

That's not all you don't talk about, retorted Lindsey silently.

An uncomfortable silence lulled between them, giving voice to the erratic thrumming of Lindsey's breathing. Her heart refused to settle on a consistent rhythm, gamboling and pirouetting like an aerobics instructor out of control.

"So." She finally drew in a breath. "When do you leave?"

"Leave?" He took a step toward her.

"Yes. For, er, Saint Andrews."

Max's brow lifted. "Oh, you know about that?"

The Electric Cupid

So you are leaving Boston, then. "Charlene told me you two were going back to Saint Andrews."

"Charlene?" He glanced at his watch. "Yes, by now, she and Thea and Brian are probably leaving the mall for the airport."

The mall? That woman she'd seen—"Well," Lindsey swallowed, struggling to keep the smile on her face. "You'd better get a move on, then."

Max frowned, confused. "Oh, we're not leaving for another week."

This time it was Lindsey's turn to be confused. "We?"

"Yes. I spoke to Harry yesterday. You didn't talk to him?" He glanced at the phone, then shook his head and sighed. "No, I suppose not. I've been trying to get a hold of you all week. I didn't bring your friend's number with me to New York, and it's been so busy at the office—"

"New York? You were in New York?"

"Yes." He sighed. "I was at a dentists' convention. I tried to call you before I left—" He paused, taking in her baffled expression. "Charlene said she called you to let you know—"

"She didn't." Lindsey shook her head. "I-I thought you'd gone back to Saint Andrews...." Her words rushed out of her mouth as he moved toward her. Her nostrils drank in his spicy, musky scent as her heart clamored noisily against her rib cage.

"Well, it wouldn't be right to go on our vacation alone." He grinned.

"Our vacation?"

Max chuckled. "Boy, you really make it tough for a guy."

"I don't know what you're talking about." She frowned. The tips of her toes and fingers were tingling.

"This is what I'm talking about." He handed her an envelope.

"What is it?"

Max cocked an eyebrow. "Open it."

She flipped open the envelope and extracted two tickets. "Plane tickets?" She read the type on the front. "To Saint Andrews?" Lindsey's mouth gaped. "But I can't—"

"I already spoke to Harry. He said it wouldn't be a problem. He seemed quite enthusiastic about it, actually.

She harrumphed. "I'll bet," she grumbled. "But listen, Max, I-I—" *I don't belong in Saint Andrews; I'll stick out like a sore thumb, and with Charlene there—*

"Oh, wait! I almost forgot." He reached behind him, scooping up a brown wrapped parcel. "I've had this under my bed for a few weeks, now. I've been holding onto it since that first time you came into the office."

Lindsey looked down at the package. "Max, I don't—"

"Go ahead, open it."

Her head was a muddied whirlpool of thoughts, and her fingers trembled as they tore open the brown paper, aware of his intent scrutiny. Why was he giving her a gift?

"The biography of Thales of Miletus!" she exclaimed, staring at the book in disbelief.

Max's grin widened. "I saw it in this little bookstore, and well, it was like I was ... I don't know—*drawn* to it for some strange reason." He gazed at her. "Now I know why."

"So you're the one who bought the book!" said Lindsey, shaking her head. "This is—" she stammered, looking up at him in a mixture of awe and bewilderment.

Max reached for her hand and entwined his fingers in hers. "You like it?"

Lindsey glanced down at their clasped hands. "Max, I love it. But—but I can't go back to Saint Andrews with you."

"You'll love it there, Lindsey. It's beautiful this time of year. We'll take my uncle's boat out onto Passamaquoddy Bay. I'll even bait your hook—"

The Electric Cupid

"I—I don't think it's a good idea, Max," she said, glancing down at the tickets in her hand. What could he be thinking? "I mean, with Charlene being there—"

"What does Charlene have to do with it?"

Anger suddenly rose in her throat. "Look, Max, this is a really nice gesture, but . . ."

"But what?"

"But you're involved with Charlene!"

Max blinked at her, first with astonishment, then bafflement. And then he suddenly threw back his head and barked a laugh. "Charlene and I? Involved? What on earth gave you that idea?"

Charlene did. "I thought—I mean, you were high school sweethearts—"

"Yes, In *high school*. Whatever there was between Charlene and me—well, that was over a long time ago."

"I think you'd better tell Charlene that," said Lindsey, thinking aloud.

Max frowned, considering for a moment Lindsey's words. "Charlene followed me here to Boston," he told her. "She thought I might need looking after, so she helped me shop for a house, helped me set up my dental practice, and appointed herself as my receptionist." He rubbed the cleft in his chin. "I never really thought . . . It was Charlene who invited Thea and Brian down here in the first place. I suppose, she was hoping they might convince me to return with them."

"So—so you're not leaving, Boston?"

"Well, only for a couple of weeks—if that's okay with you." Now their faces were only inches apart, and Max's hazel-brown eyes fastened on hers. "But no, I plan to stay right here in Boston," he said hoarsely. His gaze devoured her face, breaking off momentarily to trail down her throat, taking in her squared, defiant shoulders, her slim, solid build.

Lindsey hugged the book and tickets to her chest. "I'm glad, Max," she said quietly.

Max raked his hand through his hair, a sudden intense look contorting his features. "Lindsey McGinty, I—" He slid his hands around her. "I love you, Lindsey," he growled.

Still clutching the book and the tickets tightly to her chest, Lindsey tilted up her face to meet his, and she closed her eyes as his lips moved to claim hers. The touch of him sent a thrilling jolt through her body, and she dropped the book, the tickets fluttering to the floor.

"Oh!" she exclaimed, her hand flying to her mouth.

"Not another abscessed wisdom tooth, I hope," said Max wryly.

She grinned and shook her head. "You keep giving me electric shocks." She laughed.

"Well, you better get used to it." He cupped her face and kissed her again.

Out of the corner of her eye, Lindsey saw the arrow of the vesorium swing in their direction. She giggled, and Max followed her gaze.

"I feel like we're being watched. First that lamp of yours practically blinds me, and now that arrow contraption starts pointing at us. What is it about the two of us—"

Lindsey smiled happily and wrapped her arms around his neck. From her heart she could feel the echoing signals reaching for him, enveloping him just as she felt the echoes from his heart rush to hers and claim her for his own. She pressed her lips against his.

"It's electricity," she rasped.